# The Long Weekend

*Three days that last a lifetime*

## T. D. Henderson

# The Long Weekend

## Three days that last a lifetime

### T. D. Henderson

Compass Publishing

This edition published 2021 by
Compass Publishing
Sittingbourne, Kent, United Kingdom
www.compass-publishing.com

ISBN 978-1-912009-64-0

Design, Typeset and Production by
Jubilee Publications, Bromley, Kent, United Kingdom.

Cover Design by Juliet Storey
@jes_storeyland Instagram

Printed and bound by
Catford Printers, London, United Kingdom.

For further information, contact:
The Publisher: www.globalinstitute.org.uk
The Author: davehendersonky8@yahoo.co.uk

# Dedication

To my father with grateful thanks for giving me life.
In honour of your memory and the struggles of your
own... *'fraught little life on this incredible little
planet'.*

I dedicate this book to those courageous people who
want to explore their roots and make peace with
themselves and their history; to those who need to
find out where they came from, who they are and
where they are going.

*"The only reason why we ask other people how their weekend was is so we can tell them about our own weekend."*

*— Chuck Palahniuk*

# Acknowledgements

I acknowledge the inspiration of the one who gifted me that I might write.

Heartfelt thanks to my sister Chris who helped me growing up until I could breathe life for myself.

Special thanks also to my wonderful wife Kathryn who has been my greatest support, proof-reader, and patient encourager.

I gratefully thank my friends from the 'Learning Together Group', Jayney, Jerry and Emma, Kath and Rhoda who listened to my stories responding kindly.

Thanks also to Dr David Finch who trusted me, supported me and asked good awkward questions.

Thanks to Mark Stibbe and Malcom Down who moved me forward with editing and evaluation.

My thanks to some new friends Kathy and Loucas George who have enriched our lives and encouraged me as only good Americans can.

∞

Sincere thanks to Dr Femi Olowo and the publishing team at Jubilee Publications and Compass Publishing for your expertise, professionalism and guidance, and for making my drive to write a meaningful reality!

## Foreword

Isn't it tremendous when you find one of those books that just grips you from the very first page. You find yourself captivated by the characters and eager to know what will come to pass.

I can highly recommend The Long Weekend as one of those books.

The book is set in Yorkshire in the late 1930s and charts Rob's entry into the world of manhood. His first drink, his first experience with the divine and his first encounter with the world of women are all described with great realism and empathy. So much enfolds that I kept having to remind myself that only a weekend has passed. I am in awe as to how the author managed to pack so much into such a short span of time but then as outlined, this weekend would change the course of Rob's life forever.

The relationship between Rob and his father, is explored in depth, and we get a sense of the young Rob's deep desire to rescue his dad from the depression he is in, a responsibility too weighty for such young shoulders.

I loved the Yorkshire setting for this book and I could almost smell the stench of vinegary cockles spilled out on the pub floor during the comical scene with Rosie in the pub. These secondary characters were also intriguing for me, and I found myself fascinated by what their stories might have been. In fact the characters are so engaging that I thought at times this would make an excellent play. I certainly would love to read the next instalment and look forward to this in anticipation.

Rhoda Watters
*Teacher*
*Fife, Scotland*

-----------------------------------------------------------------

I first met Dave Henderson over 10 years ago at a workshop aimed at growing spiritual capacity.

Dave seems to have that capacity to bring out hidden treasures. In the Long Weekend he takes the reader on a journey to reclaim lost parts of ourselves, to review life with greater clarity, peace and a lot more joy.

Through the narrative a rainbow of emotions are plumbed – oxymorons, juxtapositions – a host of contradictions – yet quite clearly simple pointers to the source of greater wisdom, revealing themselves both through the central character and Dave's honesty – for those who care to look.

Emma Joylson
*A fellow traveller*

-----------------------------------------------------------------

A fantastic read with a real talent for holding the reader's attention.

Peter Carr
*Paisley*
*Scotland*

# Preface

*It was a weekend that changed my fraught little life for good. What happened over those next three days influenced the rest of my sorry time on this peculiar and fascinating little planet. They say, "in their beginning is their end." That was true for me... whoever they are.*

*It was Friday morning. "Now you're sixteen", my dad said, "you can come to the pub. Meet me there this evening after work."*

*"We can celebrate your transition from boyhood to manhood with a pint of beer."*

This is a dramatized memoir, a stirring mix of fact, fiction, and fervent imagination, about my young father's life.

If we want to know who we are, we need to look at our parents and our ancestors. We need to look closely. We need to connect with a detailed personal knowledge of their everyday lives and the culture of their times. We need to embrace them in all their good and flawed humanity. And we will discover – in some measure we are our parents, our ancestors, like it or not.

The Long Weekend is an exploration through memories and imaginings of my dad talking about his life before I came into the world.

This part of his story is set in 1938. Twelve years later when I was born, like him, I too entered into a tumultuous childhood.

I left school at 16 with a handful of 'O' levels, no common sense and no idea what to do, I bumbled through life. Home was a constant erupting volcano of anxiety. My first years of working life were unsuccessfully engaged in managing supermarkets.

After failing in marriage, I planned to take a year out and take a long hard look at my life. Fate intervened and I took another unsuccessful step and became a trainee carpenter in Warmbronn, a small village in Southern Germany. The job lasted for just five days!

My first attempt at writing my life story back in 1978 began and ended on a single A4 sheet of paper which on reading I found so depressing and boring that I abandoned the idea.

Experiencing a complete nervous breakdown at the age of 29 whilst still living in Germany, I returned to England and embraced the Christian faith. I became aware over the next four decades that I was living through a seemingly chaotic sometimes painful occasionally exhilarating journey of transformation which resulted in the liberating uncovering of my real self. And I discovered that my previously assumed identity had been significantly defined by my father. Though he was part of the picture, the unique me, the best of me, needed a lot help to emerge to the fore .

As I have been writing, I have found how fascinating it is that the effort to remember rewards. It disturbs but also heals. The process has added depth to the picture of who I really am. I discovered a me that I began to like and dislike, even though I am never mentioned in this story.

Set in Rob's home county of Yorkshire, it reveals a world far removed from our world of today.

Stepping back in time, the story reflects the spirit of an age which feels a million miles away—so far away it's almost unbelievable.

On 7th October 1938, Rob Fentiman *(not his real name)* celebrates his 16th birthday with an invitation from his dad to come to the pub and have his first official pint, to enter the world of adulthood, to become a Yorkshire version of a man.

The events of that night, and his adventures on Saturday and Sunday reveal the seeds both of his making and his undoing. Patterns woven through the next 50 years of Rob's life find their origins in this story.

Enjoy, and as my sister said to me, *'Be kind to yourself.'*

T. D. Henderson

# Contents

# 1. Boy to Man in Three Days

This weekend influenced the course of my fraught little life for good. What happened over these three days affected the rest of my time on this peculiar and fascinating little planet. They say, "In their beginning is their end"—whoever *they* are. That was true for me.

It started on Friday morning. "Now you're sixteen," my dad said, "you can come to the pub. Meet me there this evening after you've done your paper round. I'll buy yer a pint"

I did Eric's paper round, once a week after my regular work at the factory. Eric was a friend from my old schooldays.

"We can celebrate your transition from boyhood to manhood with a pint of good old Yorkshire Ale."

I was not at all sure about that. There were rows in our house over Dad's drinking. He spent so much time and money boozing it was enough to put anyone off. Most of the men round our way handed their pay packet over to their wives on Friday nights. The women were 'the Chancellors of the Exchequers', they did the budgeting, the juggling, the paying out, the figuring out how to eek things out, how to make-do to survive. Men got pocket money if they were lucky. Some men had a habit of stopping off at the pub on the way home. That was the problem. Sometimes the pay-packet never made its way to the missus in good shape.

Nonetheless you didn't argue with your dad. Going to the pub for a pint for the very first time in your life was a big deal. "It's a rite of passage," me dad said.

What it was a passage into I never understood, not till much later on. To my dad, it was a marker that I was changing status from being a boy to becoming a man. I had never been quite sure if my dad liked me or not. But with this invitation it felt like he was saying,

"You're my son. You're my lad. You're all right. Come on into the inner circle."

It was a kind of non-ceremonial, never-named, moment of bonding that cemented my entry, my belonging, to another world - the mysterious world of grownups. Once over that threshold, I would become a man. I would have arrived. I would be included in the world of adults.

So, to me, it felt like I was being brought into some kind of a fold, almost being saved from something. I was allowed into the world of men, a world which was not open to women or kids.

In his attempt to defend what seemed, on looking back, like *a chauvinistic point of view,* me dad would say, with a half chuckle, in one of his many moments of mixed-up realism and old philosophising ways.

*'The pub is a place of shelter, a hideaway from the storms and from the misery of the daily drudge. The pub is a kind of working mans' Cathedral. The saloon bar is our temple, the Ale and the bread butties are our Communion. The banter is the preaching at which we all take our turns. It's a man's spiritual restoration station. And the singing, the hymns, well, the pub songs are the anthems that bind us together. They're our mantras, our solidarity, expressing our dogmas to the rest of the world. The pub is our fortress. Being in the pub gives us the strength we need to be real men, or so we delude ourselves till we get home.'*

He would go on with...

*'Karl Marx once said that 'religion is the opium of the people'. In Yorkshire, we say the pub, the pint, and the patter are our lifeblood. That's what's kept this nation going.'*

And dad would say it with such gravity, I thought he could have been a preacher or politician himself. Neither of which would he have been pleased to be likened to.

As time went on and I looked back, I could see what he meant.

He would say things like...

*'Pubs are a place of safety from the irritation and depression of life, from being at home alone with the wife and kids, with the constant reminder that you were a failure. Home is a warzone where an enemy constantly reminds you of your flaws - an enemy who comes at you relentlessly, and from whom there is no escape.*

*If it isn't the missus having a go at you, or kids squabbling, or the endless list of undone jobs flashing their angry teeth at you from the pantry door, or the worn-out clothes and furniture, it is the sheer weight of boredom and hopelessness that gets to you. Death, the pub, or the garden shed - if you are lucky enough to have one – those are our only salvation.'*

Funny, he never mentioned God or church. I sometimes wondered about that.

That night it seemed; however, I was going 'to be saved' in the pub.

# 2. Friday 7th October 1938

So Friday night came and at half past six precisely – I headed out for my first official night at the pub. My paper round had finished later than usual; I was slow and tired. *'I must be getting old already,'* I remember thinking.

It was my sixteenth birthday, so I should have been happy, but I was haunted by a feeling that something terrible was going to happen.

The day was meant to be special. It was my sixteenth after all. I had known the day would come when I would reach that supposedly magical age. I guess I had wanted to be a man for a while now – grown-up like. The idea of it felt great. It felt like a milestone. I mean it felt like forever people had been saying – *'just you wait till yer proper grown up....'*

Well, this were it, weren't it. The day had come. But when I thought about me dad and the pub, and me mam who would nag him to death when he got home – and worse still if he were late and drunk, or if he'd spent the housekeeping on gambling, I was struggling to get too excited. She could be brutal and not just with her tongue. I guess this thought was competing for recognition in my head, fighting with the heightened emotion of anticipation, that heady mixture of fear and excitement, the uncertainty of entering manhood and all that it might mean.

The worry about it, all those confusing thoughts, got me all worked up, made me think about leaving home. Now I was sixteen, I could leave if I wanted, legally. I could get married legally and have sex legally too. Not that anybody spoke about... you know... *that*. Queen Victoria's influence still hung heavily in the air even then. The cold wind of her Puritanical prudery still blew through old England's moral catacombs. Her famous (although now often disputed) statement, *"We are not amused"* was regularly quoted in the coarse working-class alleys and backstreets of northern industrial towns and cities. Sex was a taboo subject, strictly kept under wraps, under the blankets so to speak, behind closed doors, out of 'decent' conversation. It didn't keep it out of men's hearts and minds though, women too for that matter, nor out from behind the counter in the Newsagents 'secret' publications as I discovered later on in life.

The Riveters Arms was dad's local boozer. Alongside the British Legion Club, it was the most important social hub of the town. It stood on the left-hand side on the way from home to Dorman Longs Steel Yard where Dad worked, where I worked, where just about everybody worked, or so it seemed.

Except of course for the women. Me mam worked sometimes but only when money got tight, usually at the laundry and then only part time. Married women didn't much work in them days. In the home cooking, cleaning and having kids was a wife's place back then. Unmarried women who did work tended to get jobs in assembly work in the new engineering factories that were springing up, or in the electrical, food and drink industries. Some did clerical work, typing and working in shops and that. Some young lasses worked in hospitals but by the time I was sixteen many were joining the Civil Service or even some going to college to get qualifications. The better off ones that was.

**The Rivetter's Arms**

I had never been inside the pub before—not proper like—just looking through the door some nights as it swung open and closed as men went in and out. Me mam had sent me down the road a few times to fetch dad back when she was poorly. She kept getting bouts of appendicitis—sudden attacks—bad but not bad enough for them to operate. And a few times she'd sent me out on a Friday night to make sure me dad came home with enough money to pay the rent. Friday was payday.

Being there, outside the pub, at night, was quite exciting for me, well, when I could separate my usual anxiety from excitement. I mean being there at night outside with all the hustle and bustle going on in the street, it was great. There was one night in particular I'll remember forever. It was just before mam's birthday, September time, again it was a Friday night. It was getting dark already. I was watching the Gas Lighter man coming up the street with his long lighting pole and this little lad following him around, going from lamp post to lamp post. With a flick and a flare of his magic wand he would light up the street. I watched as the flash of the gas coming to full flame chased away the darkness from the settling night sky. It was amazing. The street was so busy. I hadn't really noticed before how it was other times I had passed by on my way home from Cricket or the Boys Club.

I stood outside the pub doors that night, bathed in the mustard glow of golden light shining through the frosted glass windows etched with Fleur-de-Lys. I could hear the cheery chitter chatter of the men, and the sound of an accordion playing in the background, and the hum of voices rising and falling in soulful Irish twang as they sang out their ale-drenched version of Danny Boy, oh Danny Boy, the pipes, the pipes are calling.

Huddles of lads and lasses in the street passed by in ones and twos, some threes, older than me they seemed, and all dressed up to the nines too. There were lads with their pals, or lasses with lasses, some stepping out with their sweethearts, heading for the Roxy Cinema or the Excelsior Dance Hall no doubt, popular trysting places for courting couples in our day.

The air was filled with promise. I could feel it.

I listened to the click clack of the lasses shoes as they hurried excitedly by in their swirling dresses and smooth beige and pink coats, and their hand bags tucked under their arms. Arm in arm the lasses went by chatting and giggling, jostling along in playful armlock, high on hopefulness, swaying from side to side.

Paralysed by a momentary glance from a lass in the crowds as she turned her head and looked me in the eye, I froze. Caught off guard, trying not to stare, her flashing eyes looked right into mine. My belly jumped. The strength drained from my arms and legs.

I tried in vain to drag my eyes away from hers, embarrassed, and excited. In a rush of emotion, I was filled with a longing. Something in her took hold of me. She had something I needed. I had no idea what it was.

She pursed her lips with a mock kiss and with a swirl of her curly hair walked on, saying nothing, her eyes flashing a smile that could have charmed a thousand lads to death never mind just me.

As she disappeared out of sight the penny dropped. I flushed red.

It was Elena, Chalkie's sister. I hadn't seen her out before. Not proper, not like that. She left school a year ahead of me. My, she looked so fine, so beautiful all grown up, all dressed up 'n that. My heart swelled, and my eyes almost cried with joy.

We had played together as kids for years. When I was nine, I fell in love with her. She was so much stronger than I was. She was confident and she knew things. But kids, nine, ten years old. How do you talk of love? You don't. You just feel something; a welcome warm feeling, almost embarrassing, a mystery, you don't understand it but you hope it's shared, it stays, it lasts.

I don't know what I would have done if she had spoken to me that night though. I would have crawled between the cracks in the pavement. This past year, just thinking about girls embarrassed me to death or at least to hot flushed cheeks that I couldn't hide, even in the dark.

Thankfully she didn't stop; she walked on and was lost to sight in the crowds.

For moments I felt stranded in empty space, suspended by her eyes amidst three worlds; Elena past, Elena now, and the immediate mission to fetch dad.

I got jolted back to earth as the pub doors swung open and thumped together again. Thank God. A few men went in and out. Their chatter and bursts of laughter grabbed me back into the present and helped me climb down from my lost cloud.

Everything happened so fast.

Distracted back by the buzzing noise from the pub, I strained to get a look through the doors in the brief moments they were apart.

I was desperate for excitement too, not just for love.

My intrigue was piqued by the exhilaration of the pub's life, and I wanted to go in.

I stood outside a bit, wondering how to get my dad's attention. It was cold. I had nothing to keep me protected from the chilly night air, nothing but a thin jacket and the warm smell of fish n chips wafting up the street and the heady whiff of beer and baccy from inside the pub. But I did have my thoughts, thoughts of Elena and her smile, and those eyes, her bright flashing eyes that shone like diamonds, eyes that shone like sparkling gems, piercing eyes that burrowed and hid themselves like jewels, buried themselves in my empty sadness .

Eventually someone came through the doors I recognised, one of my dad's mates from the allotment. Rushing to grab hold of his arm I persuaded him to go and ask dad to come out. Eventually dad did and I half carried him home. It was a bit of a struggle, he was a bit reluctant, indignant even but at least he came.

**Our Street, Our Life**

Our house was no 19. It was in the middle of a row of terraced houses whose dull red bricks were crackled with age and cemented round with old, dark grey, pointing dotted here and there with crusty blobs of blackened moss like leeches sucking the life out of the houses. The unremarkable but indelible image of those red bricked walls followed me throughout life. Funny, the things that stick in your mind, ordinary things you don't suppose other people notice—everyday things that merge into a haze in the blur of mundane days. Somehow those red bricks painted their bland, yet emotive artistry upon the landscape of my long-term memory. Strange that.

Why notice, why remember, the sooty, red brick walls? I had no idea.

I guess they contributed to the sense of sadness, the oppressive black cloud that hung over the daily drudge we called life. Maybe that was it. Whatever it was, those bricks were tethered in my brain to the sense of depression and anxiety I carried through life.

So many miserable things made up that cloud; the culture of poverty, the fact that we were so low on the index of multiple deprivation which we never knew existed back then, the inequality of it all. Nobody knew how bad things were; it was just life. There was nothing else us youngsters had got to compare it with. But it still seemed wrong. It felt like it was being pressed upon us by some outside force. Nobody knew how we had all ended up in that state or who'd imposed it upon us. But somebody had and we didn't like it.

My dad used to go on about the hungry thirties, the great depression when Britain was plunged into a deep recession and there were high levels of unemployment. Workmen were angry. Very angry. He talked a lot, passionately even, about the general strike which paralysed the country and the Hunger March where workers from the more depressed areas including Tyneside and South Wales set out for London to bring their plight to the attention of the Government, a government that didn't seem to notice how bad things were. Things had never been the same since then he reckoned.

Nonetheless this heavy cloud didn't belong to us, it felt like it didn't belong to us because it shouldn't belong to anyone. Somehow, somewhere, we sensed there was an elusive better life we were meant to be living. It felt like being thirsty all the time and there was no water to be had. It just wasn't right. It had made bitter, angry men and women of us all back then. *"Those bloody Tories,"* old men would say. Everything about life which was irritating and drab and dull and hard was their bloody fault. Bloody good-for-nothing politicians!

It wasn't just the dull red bricks. There were the window frames as well, barely hanging together some of them, with layer upon layer of cracked, ancient putty hanging on with the help of several layers of green, gloss, paint, which in future years was proved to be poisonous too. They were another subliminal reminder that we were poor, hard done to, and trapped. They triggered anger and frustration in me at not being able to do a damn thing about our miserable existence. I got angry at the windows sometimes. Maybe I needed to talk to a psychiatrist after all.

I wasn't mad or crazy, but looking back, I was probably what you would now call depressed. I seemed to feel the oppression of everything. To me the windows, together with the red brick walls, were the clues that pointed to the crime of our collective oppression. And so they made me angry.

The thin glass panes of the windows seemed to mirror my own inner fragility and powerlessness. They called out to me many times to smash my fist through them. There was power in my fist. The only power I had. I half believed that doing so would get rid of the misery and the pain. I just wanted the pain and frustration to stop. But the impulse was a lie; there was no cure in that. I just needed to stop looking so hard at the windows and get my head into a better space. I knew that, but doing it was something else. Some days I couldn't.

The faded net curtains also annoyed me. They hung against the scratched glass window panes.

They were washed every week as a matter of pride - a subconscious attempt to retaliate, to assert some dignity, to protest about being poor and undervalued.

*We are going to have clean windows and clean curtains and we don't care what anyone thinks. We will be the masters of our fate. We are the captains of our soul.* (Thank you, William Henley).

Passive aggressive, or what! Really, yes many of these window panes were as cracked as their owners. Though I was just a boy, a tenant, it had gotten to me too.

We were surrounded by reminders all the time—the uneven pavement slabs that met the red brick walls in a wobbly line of mossy grime, peppered with coal dust in spite of being diligently swept and washed every week; the dogends, moodily discarded, not another decent draw to be had out of them. That is how dull and boring life was, when you sink into details like those.

Who looked at such things?

*Sad, heavy-shouldered people did.*
*Depressed people did.*
*People in need of hope did.*
*People who worked too hard, too long did.*

*People who felt trapped with no choice*
*lest they starved or*
*went on means-testing*
*for social support*
*did.*
*People who didn't*
*have enough food to eat.*
*People who couldn't*
*have new clothes,*
*or even dream of holidays.*
*People who didn't*
*have enough fuel to keep warm in winter,*
*or afford to get shoes re-heeled.*
*(We used to stuff newspapers in our shoes on wet*
*days).*
*People whose only hope*
*was coming up lucky at the bookies,*
*or somebody dying and*
*leaving you their property or possessions.*
*What a terrible thing*
*waiting for someone to die.*
*No wonder we hated our lives, ourselves.*
*We were these people,*
*people who didn't get enough sleep,*
*whose bones ached*
*in the day*

*with constant tiredness,*
*people who were starved of pleasure,*
*pleasure that didn't bite back,*
*didn't have a sting in its tail,*
*pleasure that wouldn't cause arguments*
*or poison relationships*
*already teetering*
*on the edge of disaster.*
We were the people
who noticed such things.

# 3. To the Pub with Chalkie

As I headed down the road to the pub, Chalkie White —"Charlie" on Sundays—appeared around the corner of Church Street, hands in his long, grey-flannel trouser pockets, head down, whistling at the pavement, or his feet, or to the air in front of him, oblivious of my impending presence, his mind elsewhere, or seeming to be, as always.

Chalkie and I grew up together. Went to the same school, played the same games, had the same friends, mostly. I only knew his mum and dad from infrequent visits to his house to see if he was coming out to play. His mother would often answer the door. She wore a headscarf, bundled up a bit like a turban and would be dressed in her crossover pinnie which everybody seemed to wear, the older women anyway. No idea what colour it was; drab is all I can imagine as I think back—drab, maybe light grey, or lilac, with little, hardly discernible flowers on it - daisies maybe, faint daisies, faded daisies, not long for this life, poor wilting things, washed out, fitting the mood of life perfectly.

Chalkie's sister, Elena, would be standing in the background peering over her mother's shoulder odd times I called by. Quiet then, she would be, smiling. Ever since that night she had passed me by in the street outside the pub I all but trembled when I saw her.

## Chalkie

"Hey, Chalkie! Hey up, lad! How's things? Are you ready for this?" I called out to get his attention. I had asked my dad if I could bring Chalkie along.

"Are you sure this is okay, me coming along Rob?"

"Aye, it's okay with me dad, he thought it was a good idea, said it might cheer you up"

"Why does he think I need cheering up?"

"We all do Chalkie, don't we?" Trying not to say what I was really thinking. If Chalkie had been a preacher his key theme would be "Vanity of vanities, all is vanity!"

Everything was pointless and a waste of time to Chalkie. Chalkie was the great depression in the flesh. He carried the weight of the world upon his shoulders.

He was my friend, my mate, we were close, but my, he could be heavy.

Chalkie had well-turned seventeen. He was a bit taller than me, and bigger built with boyish blonde hair. But his shoulders hunched over, like he was getting older and older more quickly than he ought.

He worked in the same factory two sheds down from me. He seemed to absorb all the dreariness of life in those great smoggy sheds with their dim lighting, oppressive airs, and acrid smells. He didn't have it in him to withstand its joy killing climate. He didn't sing, he didn't whistle, he didn't dream. The thud of life had bashed him into stultification and deadness.

His boyishness was in his face and boyish blond hair, but it had gone missing from his heart long since. Bombarded on every side of life with hard to bear stuff like most of us were, he rarely found a way to rise above it. When he did, it was a brief encounter with happiness that barely went skin deep and was soon forgotten.

He went to work at 6.45 o'clock in the morning. His team worked the early shift as well. Some of the older men were in there already, some already drunk, past trying to hide their bottles of hooch wrapped in old greasy newspaper stashed in their overalls, or the front pouch of their leather aprons, singing filthy songs with  glints in their eyes, not hiding their well engrained sense of hopelessness or the beyond-caring—anger in their guts. They were like mountain ranges of volcanos just waiting for the right reason to explode, beyond caring about the consequences. Their anger was their stored-up weapon of last resort, carried in them as a kind of suicidal death wish, the only thing they had left in them for their way out of the endless cycle, the pressure cooker of monotony, the weight of boredom, the cavern of joyless living death they were born into, a cavern whose darkness they were forced to fumble through every repetitive muscle tiring, draining day. They were just waiting for the wrong person to give them the right reason to erupt.

Chalkie breathed that poisonous air into his soul day after endless day. Those were the toxins that killed his potential, the dry worthless death food served up daily, the negative nourishment that wormed its way into the bones of his premature growing oldness.

We all felt the heaviness of life, but Chalkie more so. Chalkie could rarely find an ounce of joy. Chalkie, my friend, my self-selected surrogate brother, my fellow life-journeyman was heavy. He was a ton of bricks more often than not.

It was the devoidness of imagination that killed him, not the final expiration of air from his lungs, not the eventual cessation of his heartbeat but his inability to see beyond his house, his street, that factory. Some quirk in the workings of his mind, something in him had killed any real capacity for joy he ever had. He couldn't seem to rise up and breathe the clean fresh life-giving air of pleasure. He was blind to the simple beauty in the world. If he ever had any curiosity in him, it was dead. Devoid of imagination he couldn't see the possibility of another life. There was beauty and life still to be found but you had to fight for it—seek it out and grasp it with both hands whenever it happened your way. Chalkie hadn't the fight; except when it came to football.

As he thought, so he was. Vanity, vanity, all is vanity, saith the preacher—life was a total waste of time. Chalkie didn't say it with words, he oozed it with feeling. And he was only seventeen.

He hadn't gotten invited to the pub by his dad, ever.

**Chalkie's dad**

His dad was a waste of space; never did anything with his kids, except grunt, grumble, and wave his fist in the air. Occasionally, if some irritating neighbour complained about them, you would have seen him out on the street, braces twisted over his shoulders, frown fixed even tighter than normal, grubby white collarless shirt, sleeves rolled up to the elbows, snorting blue murder, grabbing Chalkie by the lug, pulling him "ouching" lurching, staggering at the end of his father's rough strong arm, back inside the house to get some kind of a leathering.

*"I was only mucking about,"* I would hear Chalkie protesting. *"Just a bit of fun, Dad."*

Wallop.

*"Ouch! That hurt."*

Wallop again.

*"Ouch! Stop it, Dad! I didn't mean no 'arm."*

Wallop again and then a whimpering cry from Chalkie and some smart justifying comment from his dad. Then I would hear Chalkie's voice gradually fading as he ran up the stairs, and the rumble of him tripping on the steps as he clambered into the back bedroom. I imagined him flinging himself face-down on the bed for a feeling-sorry-for-himself whimpering and a bit of mumbled cursing over his stupid, heartless dad.

Chalkie's mum never did anything about it. She just cowered in the scullery or the washhouse while it went on. Maybe she thought she'd get a leathering too. Though I never heard of him walloping her or Elena for that matter. Men didn't hit women, mostly.

There were occasionally rumours running around of maybe a few men in particular taking things out on their women folks, especially weekends, pub nights. But it were frowned upon. I heard me dad talk about it to others sometimes. But marriages were sacrosanct – he would say, you don't interfere between a man and his wife – if you knew what was good for yer.

We'd walked on a few hundred yards. The pub was only ten minutes from our house.

'So what you been up to Chalkie?'

'Nowt much. Just the usual. Working, doing me chores, fetching the coal and tidying up the back garden. I had me football practice on Monday and Wednesday. We've got another big match coming up next month.'

The one thing that brought Chalkie alive was football. Not so much talking about it, or even going to watch matches, but playing football. If ever you saw a transformation in a person, you'd see it then when Chalkie was playing. And he was good as well. He stood a chance of getting chosen for the county team.

'Sunday is just a local game though, Denmark Street against Cannon Street South. They are a tough bunch, but we'll beat them easy.'

Like I said, Chalkie came alive when it came to his football. His usual heavy pessimism disappeared, and like water turning into wine, his spirits lifted, he was another person altogether.

We turned the corner onto Newport Road. We could have gone down Cannon Street but found it best to avoid it on a Friday night. It was a pretty rough place at the best of times and Chalkie didn't want to run into any of the opposition before the game on Sunday. He didn't trust them if he was seen, not to come and rough him up a bit. Foul play was fair play to the Cannonites.

The Pub we were going to tonight was on the corner of Calthorpe Street and Spencer Street, just up the road from Marsh Road School.

There was a notice board on the pavement outside DiCarlo's Newsagents and Tobacconists carefully positioned so you had to walk round it.

### *'RECESSION LIFTS, WAR LOOMS'...*

...was the roughly written message as the headlines of the day. I ignored it. It was Friday night and me birthday. I didn't want to think about anything.

At the next corner of Harris and Hartington a number of older lads and lasses were mulling around outside the cinema, no doubt waiting for their date. We shuffled passed them, head down as though trying to hide, pretending not to look at them, but darting a sideways glance at the lasses, inwardly wanting to look on what felt like their happiness. At least I did. Chalkie didn't give much away.

# 4. Entering the Realm

Suddenly we were there. We arrived at the pub. We opened the double swing doors together, slowly pressing the big brass handles forward, making our timid entrance onto the hallowed stage of promised new life. The doors were dark mahogany, shiny varnished, with glass panels etched with motifs and the pub's name, 'The Rivetters Arms'. I didn't know what the gallows would have felt like, but we were nervous and excited. Once inside we stood still and just looked. Peering through the smoky blue air, I saw me dad sitting on the bench on the left, dominoes in his hand, chappin' on the brown varnished table in front of him.

"Okay, Bill. It's your turn," he says to his partner.

He looked up and clocked us as we began to edge forward in his direction. He saw us before the barman did, fortunately, or he'd have given us what for.

"Come on in, son. Come over here. You too, Chalkie." He turned to the barman. "It's okay Walter, they're with me." Then back to us. "Grab a pew, lads." He half grunted a friendly welcome, faintly smiling.

We edged our way nervously between the tables and chairs in the middle of the bar and headed towards me dad.

"Right then, what will it be, lads? I think you lads should have a pint of light. A pint of heavy would be too much for you to start with. An' Chalkie, are you sure your dad's not going to fall out wi' me if he finds out?"

"He won't find out, Mr Fentiman," Chalkie says. "If you don't tell him."

"I won't, son," Dad replies. "Don't you worry about that. He won't find out from me. Mum's the word."

I felt an odd, frightened sensation when he said the word *"mum."* Funny how a single word conjures up an encyclopaedia of thoughts and emotions, how that simple word *"mum"* had the power to freeze my heart, paralyse my mind and transfix my body, like a warning of impending doom.

I shook off my paralysis and looked around the bar. The air across the pub was thick with smells – the mini marauding cloud of tobacco smoke competing with the bitter-sweet aroma of freshly poured beer, the salt-and-vinegar tang from the cockles and whelks, the unwelcome odour from the stale mop that got waved across the floor after the lunchtime stampede, the waft of Jeyes sanitary block from the gents out the back.

Pipe tobacco had the strongest smell, pungent and unavoidable. It grabbed your nostril's attention with its host of exotic aromas. It had a funny way of touching you somewhere deep down. Maybe it reminded me of Grandad Pennuck, mother's dad. He was a lovely old man. He liked his pipe. It was calming, reassuring. It made me feel warm and somehow managed to tickle my laughing reflexes. I found myself grinning at the first whiff.

Funny that.

I never understood why smells, words and images seemed to affect us so much.

Like the smell of pipe tobacco.

Or the word, "mum".

# 5. Getting Stuck In

Dad came back from the bar, skilfully managing three pints clasped together in his gnarled hands.

"There you are lads," he says, as he sets the glasses down in the middle of the table. "Get that down you and see what you make of it. Oh, and happy birthday, son. Here's to your good health lad. And you too Chalkie."

"Well son, you've got your whole life ahead of you. Now you're a man, things are gonna change."

We all took a good, hearty swig, all manly like, me and Chalkie, licking our lips to signal we enjoyed it.

"What do you reckon, Chalkie? Drop of alright or what, eh?"

I looked to him for reassurance.

"Yeh, great stuff. Alright, eh!"

To be honest, I wasn't too keen. It was a bit bitter. But I figured it would grow on me. Yorkshire beer was the pride and joy of the county, well one of them. Yorkshire folk had got a lot of pride in a lot of things. If I said I didn't like the beer there would have to be something wrong with me, beer never lies, and I didn't want to get chucked out of adulthood just when I was getting started.

I wasn't sure if Chalkie was being honest about the beer, but he wasn't going to let on if he wasn't either. After all, me dad and all these men seemed to like it, a lot. Maybe that's what it was to be a man. Stiff upper lip an' all that. Don't let anything bother you. Make out everything is fine. As the night went on I began to realise it was probably wasn't the taste so much as the effect it had on them they liked.

I don't know why, but at this point I asked me dad,

"Why is the drinking age 16? Why do we have to wait till now? Well I know Chalkie is 17 already, and this is his first but apart from that?"

"Well as far as I understand it, you can drink at home as a kid from when you're five if your parents are around.

*"Five"*, I burst out!

Me dad carried on regardless.

"But they reckon it affects your brain in a bad way if you drink alcohol when you are too young."

He takes a sip and goes on to say,

"I was reading in the Yorkshire Post the other week an article by the West Riding Temperance Society. They reckon your brain doesn't grow properly if you start too soon, say it affects your memory. He chuckled. I know that's bloody true. I can't remember a damn thing some mornings if I've had a skinful the night before. I'm tellin' you. You can't think properly neither."

We all took another sip. We didn't know if we should laugh or not.

"Your grandad Pennuck, your mam's dad, got cirrhosis of the liver and died at 54 cos of it. Reckon in his day nobody cared that much how young you were. Trouble was he got addicted to it and couldn't get by a day without a drink they reckoned. He'd get the shakes. It affects yer hormones as well when you're growin' up, they say. It can make you moody and a bit, you know what I mean, lads?"

He winks with a wry smile. He nudges me with his elbow. I flushed and looked down.

"When I was a lad, you could get a drink in a pub at 13, but there were that many kids getting blotto and ending up in hospital with accidents, so they decided to change it. They reckoned if you were a bit more grown up you would be more sensible and not drink so much. Bit daft logic, I say. Look at us old yins when we've had a skinful. We have less accidents cos we've learnt how to stagger without fallin' off the pavement. "

We laugh.

"Yep, expert staggerers we auld yins are. Plenty of practice, that's what does it."

More laughter all round.

There were more arguments over drink in our house than anything else, so listening to this as well, I thought to meself,

*'What the bloody hell were we doing here? What was this madness all about? What were we doing here getting initiated into something that could ruin our brains, shut down our memory banks, pickle our livers and cause havoc at home?'*

Little did I know, that was exactly what it would do to me in the years to come. In spite of that, after another couple of swigs, I was beginning to like it, and I was barely halfway down the first pint.

# 6. The Night Begins in Earnest

Just as I was beginning to enjoy the slightly heady lightness that was coming over me, the Salvation Army came through the doors.

"Here's the Sally Ann," some of the men shouted. "Mind your language lads. There's respectable company about now."

There were two of them looking just the business in their dark blue uniforms - a man and a woman, well, a girl really. Often it was two women I had seen out and about on the streets. It was easier to recruit women apparently. The Salvation folks figured they were more sensible and less likely to get tempted by "the demon drink", to use the term back then. Not sure that was true, but this one must have seen the light, and the fella too I suppose. They would go round the pubs, selling their magazines, trying to get us daft working men to see sense, to give up the booze, so I found out as they started chatting to us. I wondered why the landlord had let them in; surely it wasn't good for business—persuading people not to drink?

The noise in the pub seemed to quieten down as they came around the tables with their *War Cry* magazine. A lot of tables took one without fuss and handed over the penny they asked for in return. We all knew it was in a good cause. They used the money to set up orphanages and places for homeless people, giving them a bed for the night and some grub in their bellies. But they had to listen to that Bible stuff first; that was part of the deal. The preacher had to have his say. *'It's no good saving the body if you don't save the soul,'* or so they said, although I'm not too sure what they meant by saving. Maybe I should've asked.

There was something special about those folks - a kind of a quiet goodness. I wish I'd paid more attention back then and thought a bit more about why.

As if on cue, just as I was thinking that the young Salvation lass came over to our table.

"Oh, here's yer chance, Chalkie," me dad says, nudging him this time.

"Would you like a magazine?" she asked softly looking me straight in the eye. I don't want to exaggerate but it was as if an angel had spoken, I'm not kiddin yer. Honestly, it was something else. I could hardly speak, it was so, I don't know, well lovely, so beautiful, her voice, it melted something inside me.

*I thought it must be my age, what with Elena's eyes just the other week and now this angel voice wreaking havoc with my emotions, what was going on?*

The Sally Anne lass can't have been more than 18. How had she gotten involved with this lot? I thought to mesel *('myself' in proper English they told me when I eventually left Yorkshire).*

I was spared a few minutes to get a grip of mesel by dad chipping into the conversation.

"I'd rather have a donut," he says.

I thought he was being daft or disrespectful or summat. He never had much good to say about church folks at home. *'Right bunch of do-gooders,'* he would say.

"Dad! What are you saying?"

She turned her head to him. *"What do you mean?"* she asks. She was faintly blushing, not quite sure of his angle.

"You're too young to know, I guess," he answered. Then continued. "Back in the war, about 250 of you lot went over to France to take supplies to the soldiers. Risked their lives, they did, all dressed up in their uniforms, traipsing through the trenches, up to their garters in mud."

Me dad takes a sip. I blushed again, proper like this time. Why did he have to say garters?

"They would cook donuts for the soldiers using their metal army helmets."

She and Chalkie and me looked at him a bit unbelieving.

"True as I'm sitting here in front of you now" he says, "Heated the helmets up and cooked the donuts in oil on the little gas stoves they carried around with them. The Yanks liked donuts; you see. Trying to lift their spirits a bit they were. Good of them really. Though I wasn't much taken with the Yanks meself. Show offs. Everything bigger and better back home, they bragged a lot. And they were always trying to get off with our lasses, trying to tempt them with nylons and chocolates and Wrigley's Chewing gum, can you believe it"

Taking him at his word, though still a bit skeptical she pushes on…

"No donuts tonight, sir. I'm sorry," she says. "But we do have our magazine and there are some good articles in it, you know. Lead you to a better life they will. Might even save your soul too if you're willing!"

"Will it save me going down to them blinking murderous coke ovens at six o'clock Monday morning, lass?"

"No, I don't suppose it will do that. But it is in a good cause, to help really poor people, people with nowhere to live and no food or work. Orphans too."

Me dad gives in and hands over the penny.

"Thanks, Private Smith," he says, reading the badge on her lapel. "You're a good salesman, lass. Keep up the good work."

She thanks him, looks from face to face at me and Chalkie, then moves on to the next table. Fifty years on and I can still see that face, that smile and still feel the echoes of that angelic voice.

"Okay lads," me dad says. "Where were we? Let's get back to the serious business of drinking. You ready for another one, Rob? What about you Chalkie?"

"Not just yet, Dad. I'm only halfway down this pint. I'm not used to it yet. I should probably take it steady on me first night."

I was trying to be sensible. I know my dad could get carried away with the beer once he got going, at least judging by the state of him when he would eventually get home some nights. Specially Friday night and this was a Friday night.

"Okay, son. We've got plenty of time yet, plenty of time."

He looked at Chalkie's glass and must have figured he was about the same mind as me. He goes up to the bar and buys himself another.

"Well, what do you think Chalkie?" I ask. "You okay mate? You're a bit quiet. Everything alright?"

I don't know why I said that he was always quiet.

"Yeh, I'm fine. Can't help thinking what me dad will do if he smells the booze on me when I get back."

"Don't worry about that, he'll have to get used to it. You're well of age now. You're a year older than me."

# 7. Rosie Cheeks

We sat there, the two of us, quiet for a bit, looking around amused whilst dad was up at the bar. The nerves had settled down and my cheeks felt cooler.

A strong smell of fishy vinegar began wafting around us, stronger than normal. I felt a nudge in the middle of me back.

"Ooops! Sorry, lad!"

Someone had bumped into me. I nearly choked on me pint and my teeth bashed on the glass.

"Ouch! Mind yersel, can't yer!" I blurted out. "What are you up to anyway? What's that smell?"

I looked round to see who it was and put my pint down at the same time. My face broke into an involuntary grin as a pair of rosy-red cheeks smiled a beaming great smile at me.

"It's the cockles and whelks you're smellin'," says the cheeky imp who'd dug her elbow in me back. "You want to buy a poke or two? You must be hungry now after all that beer."

"What do you mean *'all that beer'*? This is me first and I haven't finished this one yet."

I was stuttering the words out and trying not to blush again.

The girl was dressed a bit rough but my, she was a pretty one, so she was. Bright flashin' eyes she had, like folks who work on the land or on the sea. Not like the deadened glaze you would see in the eyes of most folks around our town - the foundry workers especially with the look of deep tired sadness in their souls. This lass looked alive with her fine, auburn hair under her navy-blue beret. Maybe no older than me she was neither.

"How much are they, anyway?" I asked, trying to sound composed and grown up. "Can you eat them just like that?"

"Of course, you can. They're cooked first then soaked in vinegar. You'll love 'em. Go on have one each. They're only a halfpenny a poke. Treat yerselves. I heard someone say it was your birthday. Go on. Go on."

I was unable to resist. I was starving. I had only had a bit of bread at lunchtime and that was it since morning. I didn't get much for breakfast either - a slice of bread n' drippin and a skinny bit of sausage. That was it, every Friday. We were Church of England. Glad we weren't Catholics. I wouldn't fancy sardines for breakfast.

We gave our little fishy friend a halfpenny each and took a poke.

I had cockles and Chalkie took the whelks.

I didn't know what to do about me dad. He was still at the bar chattin' away to his mates.

"Who told you it was me birthday anyway?" I asked, more composed now, trying to get the lass to stay a bit longer and chat. "Why would anyone tell you that? You don't know me, do you?"

She pointed to our dad.

"Him," she said. "He was teasing me, asking what a pretty young girl like me was doing trudging round bars doin' this. I should be out dancing and courting at my age, he says. I don't have a fella, I tell him. I've never seen one I liked enough. He pointed over to you and says, what about him - that lad there, the good lookin' one with the mousy hair? Go n' chat him up, he says. You never know your luck."

"I'm not doing that I told him. I'll get a reputation". Go on! He says, it's his birthday. Give him a little birthday kiss, he says, and you'll make his day. So that's how I know. But don't go getting any ideas, there will be no kiss from me tonight. Enjoy your cockles, anyway."

She turned to go. Fuelled now with more beer for courage, I stood up as fast as I could, tapped her on the shoulder, leaned over the table to give her a surprise kiss, and bloody well nearly fell headlong. She turned back to face me as I tried to give her a peck on the cheek. But she was too quick for me, she pulled away and I went crashing down. I landed flat out on the table, knocking my glass for six and spilling the rest of me drink. Fortunately, Chalkie had his glass firmly in his hand and his whelks in the other. My cockles went for a burton though with what was left of me beer. What a mess, I ask yer! Rosie cheeks giggled a right girly laugh and waltzed off.

"I told you, lad," she says bemused, looking back at me over her shoulder. "I told you there would be no kiss from me tonight." She chuckled to herself as she made her way to the next customer.

Talk about embarrassed. I didn't know where to put myself. Everybody in the pub was looking in my direction wondering what had happened. Me dad returned to the table wondering as well. Elsie the barmaid shouted across the bar as I stood there like a lemon wondering what to do.

"Leave that to me lad! I'll clear that up in just a jiff!"

I hadn't seen there was a barmaid before, but I was grateful she came to my rescue. In a swish or two, she had the table wiped and the floor cleared of its broken glass and fishy mess, although the smell lingered and got right up my nose. Spilt beer, cockles, whelks and vinegar, a stale bleachy mophead, along with wisps of Gold Flake pipe smoke and a woodbine or two to add a bit of bounce to it all, not exactly air for whetting yer appetite.

On his way back to our table with his pint, dad spouted out with a touch of good-hearted chiding. "That'll teach you to get fresh, lad. Drink gone to your head already, eh? Never mind. No harm done. You'll maybe catch her next time round. Ha, ha. Let's get yer another pint now and move over to the next table."

I must admit I was surprised at how well he had taken it. I half expected him to get mad at me, but he seemed genuinely trying to make sure I had a good time. Chalkie looked on, bemused, annoyed, puzzled, not quite knowing what to make of me. This was a new situation for both of us. How were we as adults now supposed to act?

It was turning out to be quite an adventure.

# 8. Talk of War

Dad ordered the beer and the barmaid brought it over to the neighbouring table where we relocated. Someone had left a copy of the South Yorkshire Gazette. Me dad picked it up and began to read. His eyes came to rest intently on one of the inside pages. He froze. It was like he had come to a standstill and couldn't move. Me an' Chalkie both noticed it and looked at each other.

'What's up, Dad? What have you seen?"

"Nothin' at all. It's nothin'."

But his mood had changed. He went cold and looked troubled.

"It must be something, Dad. What is it? Come on tell us."

The beer must have given me courage; I wouldn't normally talk to me dad like that. We didn't talk that much at all usually.

"It's Germany and that madman Hitler. He's gone and invaded Czechoslovakia. That means certain war for us. I'm telling you. We'll be at war before long, you mark my words. War, I'm telling you, and it's not twenty years since the last murderous bloody bloodbath of a war finished. It's not something I would ever want to live through again."

Dad took a gulp of his beer.

"I'm telling you, lads. War is on the way. That lunatic Hitler is trouble. He won't stop in Czechoslovakia either. He wants to take over the world. At least our world. I don't care what that idiot Chamberlin says. 'Peace in our time,' my bloody backside. You just wait and see, lad. You had better get yersels prepared. It's comin' as sure as I breathe. God help us, more bloody misery an killin'. Oh God, no wonder we're driven to drink."

He saw that we were looking a bit confused.

A heavy minute passed in silence, till dad picked himself up again.

"Sup up lads. Let's enjoy ourselves while we can. Sorry, son, sorry Chalkie. I didn't mean to spoil your night lads. It just shook me when I read it. Truth is, I can't understand why nobody in here has said anything about it either. Surely others have read the papers as well."

I remembered we'd seen something outside the newspaper shop about *'War Looming'*. I thought it just meant the workers and the government again, I didn't really understand it. I'd heard some men talking odd times about the war of 1914-18 and how horrible that was and how many young men had lost their lives, millions slaughtered they said. But that was all before I was born.

Dad turned to a friend of his.

"Cedric!" he shouted over to a nearby table. "Have you read the Gazette today?"

"No. Why? What's in it? Have you seen a good tip for the races at Redcar tomorrow? Gonna win the tote and retire, are we?"

Cedric must have sunk a few already. He was a bit free with his mouth.

"No, not that, Cedric I'm serious now. That bit about that maniac Hitler in Germany."

"What's wrong with him?" Cedric replied. "He's for the working man, isn't he? Good labour politics, looking out for the working classes, people like us I reckon. He'll do them proud and us a bit too I reckon. You wait and see."

"Okay," my dad replied. "If he's such a bloody saint, then why has he just sent his troops across the border to invade his neighbours? How's that helping the working men over there, or us for that matter? You know we've got a treaty with the Czechs to defend them if they're attacked, don't you?"

A quietness descended in the bar.

"You know what this means don't you? This means you and me 'ill get called up to go in and get the bastard out of there. Bloody Nora, another bloodbath, mark my words."

He paused for a bit, a few seconds maybe.

"Thank God these lads are too young. I just hope we can sort it out before they get old enough to join up. Don't you remember what happened in the last war, Cedric?"

There was silence. Everyone up our end of he pub was listening now.

"Do you know how many of our young lads were slaughtered or maimed, came home with half a body missing and out of their minds, some of them? Half the young folks in the County were wiped out. Cricket teams were nigh on obliterated and half the football league into the bargain. I think Middlesbrough lost half their squad. And the League fixtures were cancelled for four years. They reckon there were more civilians killed than soldiers to boot. We've never been the same since that war none of us, and I don't want these lads going through that like we did."

"Sorry, I wasn't thinking," Cedric says. He had sobered up a bit now. "I never got called up you know. I've got this heart problem, so I stayed at home. I was in the Home Guard, so I never had it like you did. Tha's never really spoke much about it before Tom. I guessed it must have been pretty hairy though. I know you said you were lucky to survive."

A number of the other men listening in added their murmurs of confirmation and nodding ayes to the now open public conversation.

"And you used to have horrible nightmares for years after, I heard you say."
Albert, his friend from the allotment and some of the others on the side seats chipped in with various comments...

"Aye, I've never been the same since", says he.
"I'm still waking up sweating and screaming me missus tells me." Another chipped in.
Then another "I can see their blackened faces and sunken white eyes every waking day.
It's little wonder we drink ourselves daft carrying memories like that."
"Do you really think it'll come to another war, Tom?"
"By Christ, I hope not," Cedric, "I hope not."

# 9. A Gloom Descends

The mood in the pub changed, as if a black cloud had descended upon us. The prospect of war brought a chill to our hearts. You could feel it in the air, almost touch it. Chalkie and I looked on a bit bewildered. We had never seen men like this before. So many of the men in the bar were old enough to have lived through the war. I had heard me dad talk about it but only occasionally, and we had been taught a bit about it at school, but not much.

Then there were those magazines you came across. '*I Was There*' they were called, wi' loads o' pictures of tanks and planes and bombs and soldiers and ships and subs and that. To us kids, it was just a bit of harmless excitement. And it all seemed way in the past, history even though it was just 20 years ago. To us that was more than a lifetime. It didn't seem real. Like in our comic books—a bit of fun, a game.

I can't say the same for the Great Depression, though, as me dad and others called it. They often talked about those days—when we were still in short trousers.

"Those were days where we knew real hardship," they said. "No work, no food in the pantry, precious little beer either. Fags and baccy hard to come by. A good feast was a slice of bread and drippin'—and a

MacFarlane Lang's digestive biscuit wi' a cup o' sweet tea as a special treat on a Saturday. Sunday dinner was scrag end o' lamb wi' a few potatoes and Yorkshire pudding filled with onion and thin gravy like water. Thank God for Yorkshire pudding. It probably saved us from becoming skeletons."

All that was not long after I had left primary school in the early 1930s. I'd have been about nine or ten.

"Here we are now just coming out of those dark clouds," me dad said sounding like he was almost crying.

"And this killin' gloom has descended on us again." Us lads could feel it. We didn't really understand it, but we knew it were bad.

"What happened to the good old days of the 1920s?" me dad says.

"What happened to the music and dancing and Scott Fitzgerald and easy living? What happened to the peace and prosperity they promised? 'The war is over now,' they said—'the war to end all wars,' they said. 'That's it! There will never be another one like it.' They promised that impossible promise we all wanted to believe. Like any politician's promise though, not worth the paper it's written on, not worth the breath it took to say it."

He stared again at the table.

"Bloody hell!" me dad burst out, like he'd just woken up in a sweat from a nightmare.

"It will be bloody hell on earth again for sure. Can't they give us a break these damned politicians? We don't want to fight. It's their bloody fight, always squabbling about summat."

He sighed.

"An' it's us innocent civilians that pay the price, decent working folk like ourselves asked to carry out indecent damned orders to kill and murder other men and women just like us, ordinary hard-working people trying to get on wi' their lives as well, make an honest livin' like us and mind our own bloody business. Why can't they toffs do the same? Always squabblin' about summat..."

I think we would all have cried with him, if we had seen even one teardrop fall from his still blackened cheek. I don't think I ever saw him quite so emotional. But it seemed like he was pitching all the strength he could muster to keep back the tears, his own, hard-earned teardrops. Everything within him strained to keep his composure, to be a man. For men didn't cry. Yet the world deserved those teardrops, the world needed them, needed them, but never got to see them. If the world could have seen the weeping already in men and women's hearts back then, they might never have gone to war. Surely there was enough pain to contend with in life without it.

*'Why don't men cry?'* I thought.

I did. Mind you, it was under the blankets.

*'Do I have to stop now I am a man?'* I wondered.

# 10. Rescued by the Band

As Dad sank deeper and deeper into gloom, I interjected in an effort to cheer him up. "Come on, Dad. Let's have a game of dominoes."

It didn't seem much like a happy birthday anymore. More like "the sentence of death day."

The words were barely out of my mouth when, 'ecky thump, the rousing sound of music began to fill the air. It drew closer and closer and louder and louder until, through the swing doors, came the blast of the North Riding Miner's Brass Band. They marched in as if on cue, disrupting our miserable conversations about the war. Proper rousing it was, powerful stuff, tremendous, the five of them blowing away on the trumpet and bassoon, there was a trombone an' all, a Cornet, and French Horn. They were playing 'A British Grenadier.' They must have heard us lamenting from a distance.

*'Some talk of Alexander and some of Hercules, of Hector and Lysander and such great names as these, but of all the world's great heroes there's none that can compare with the tow, row, row, row, row, row, row, to the British Grenadier.'*

"Oh my God," me dad says. "More war music. There's no escaping it, I guess. Fate is fate."

Dad dived into his second pint, thrusting it down his throat to drown out the anguish that had taken hold of him.

"Bloody Hell! Bloody Hell! That's what it will be!"

Pulling himself together with the help of the best part of a stiff pint downed in a oner, "Come on lads," he said, finishing off the last drop.

"Let's have another and see if we can get these doomsayers to play us something more heartening before we drown ourselves in sorrow and woe."

The feisty five moved over to the corner near the piano. They must have sensed a negative mood. The lead man asked, "Any requests, men? You look like you need cheering up."

At this point, the night could easily have descended into a row about war, dragging up more old wounds, stirring up fears, bitterness and resentment. It could easily have become ugly. Maybe the band was a godsend, sent to distract us. The men were definitely glad of a reason to change the subject and move on, not wanting to think about the idea of war anymore until they had to. After all, it wasn't absolutely certain yet. Denial was always the first port of call, the first hideout when something nobody wants to face comes knocking at your door. Pretend it's not there and maybe it'll go away. Well it did go away for a bit anyway.

One of the men in the pub spoke up. "It's Friday night, lads. Come on! Let's have a good old singsong and cheer ourselves up. We've all worked hard, and we've earned it! And mind, no more war songs. We need our souls soothing and saving not savaged and slaughtered."

There was a murmur of approval.

"What'll it be then?" Henry the band leader asks.

"Play *'Over the Rainbow'*, Henry!" one of the men shouted. "I love that Judy Garland! She's a proper brammer, so she is. Voice like an angel. She could sing me to sleep with a lullaby any day of the week. Well maybe only Thursdays when the misses is away at her mother's"

A ripple of laughter shimmied though the atmosphere. Things began to lighten up.

The band started up. Judy Garland won the day as a pub full of admiring dreamers sang along to her imaginary presence. Practically the whole pub joined in, led on by the boys with the brass. These men could sing as well. I guess we'd all had a few by then. It was about 9 o'clock and the Rivetters Arm's male voice choir (and Elsie the barmaid of course) bursts into great crescendos of song. Deep, soulful, heartfelt stuff it was too. Boy, did it change the mood. I don't know if we all wanted to drown our sorrows in song, but it was bloody marvellous, so it was. 'This was more like it,' I thought to meself.

The men across the bar shouted out their favourite tunes.

"How about *'Cheek to cheek'* by Fred Astaire? He's a terrific turn too. That'll get us all going." Or *'These Foolish things.'* That's another cracking song. He's some singer that Benny Goodman. I heard him on the radio just the other week. Terrific. What a crooner! No, l tell you what, how about *'Happy Days are here Again?'* That should do the trick!" The men across the bar shouted out their favourite tunes.

The band played and played for what seemed like ages. We were in a kind of dream by the finish, high as kites and gaspin' wi' thirst. It must have been good, we'd stopped supping all the time we were singing.

Henry, the bandleader, called the band to a halt and made an announcement. "That was just a taster lads and lasses, well Elsie anyway. We came in to remind you that the concert is on tomorrow afternoon at the Bandstand in Starbank Park at 2 o'clock. It's a fundraiser for the poorhouse in Church Street, so do come along and join us. It's all in a good cause, and the way things are looking we might all end up in there some day."

Henry took a breath and continued.

"Come and support us men, and wear those old overcoats, the ones with the deep pockets an' all. There is a lot of folks much worse off than ourselves, so get home safe and don't kick the milk bottles on the front doorstep or if you're sneaking round the back mind not kick the tin bath or you'll wake the missus and there will be hell to pay."

There was laughter all around the room.

"Thanks Henry!" the men shouted out as the musicians headed out the door playing a modern rendition of a much-loved song.

*'Pack up your troubles in your old kit bag and smile, smile, smile. What's the use of worrying, it never was worthwhile, so, pack up your troubles in your old kit bag and smile, smile, smile.'*

Okay, it was a reminder of the War, but it was a good lively tune, and the words helped us all to think not to worry so much. It helped keep the spirits up, fortified us, kept us going. "A man's got to have summat uplifting in life or it would crush us completely." Dad would say.

# 11. Lady of the Night

As the doors closed behind the band and things went quiet, I noticed a woman standing just inside the door by the entrance. She had her back to the wall, one foot raised behind her, stiletto pressed flat against the wood panelling and her bent knee showing out of her red skirt beaming at us like the headlight of a car. But she was quiet, just standing still, smiling. She wore black high heels and black nylons with a thin black line up the back of her leg. You could just about see from where I was sitting and looking, if I twisted my neck around. She reminded me of the girl in the poster at the cinema and that caption:

*'I'm not perfect, but parts of me are incredible.'*

Oo, la, la. I couldn't take my eyes off her.

"Are you listening, young un?" I heard me dad say, a bit loud like. "Are you wanting another pint before we head off home? What's that you're gawpin' at?"

He followed my line of vision across the room and clocks the flaunting looker at the doorway.

"Get yer eyes off her, me lad! She's trouble, I'm warning yer. Take my word for it."

Walt the barman spots her about the same time. He calls out to her in a slightly hushed voice, trying to be a bit discrete. "Come on, Mavis. You know you're not allowed in here love. Make yerself scarce before I call the boys in blue."

Fat lot of good that would do, as I was about to find out.

Mavis moved away from the wall swishing her fur coat from side to side. It was open at the front. She had her chest pushed out and her red skirt swirled around over her hips.

She walked confidently up to the bar; her cheeky little nose pointed her strawberry blonde head up in the air. She was smiling, brazen as you like.

"Alright, Walter. If that's what you want."

She turned right around and glided back to the swing doors. I swear she was walking on air. She cast a cheeky glance across the room, pouting her lips with her eyes flashing, looking to catch a hungry soul with her magic spell.

And off she went.

I'm sure she took my heart or something with her.

"What was all that about?" I asked no one in particular, still trying not to show that my heart was beating faster than a soldier's drum. Chalkie had his head down. He was lookin' a bit embarrassed or something. He had a sheepish grin on his face. That was a rare sight, I didn't often see him smile. Me dad had gone off to the bar to get us a drink. He was on his way back, this time a bit less stable on his feet.

"There you are me lads. Happy days!"

"Who was that dad? Is she a film star? I've seen posters with girls like that outside the cinema but never seen one in the flesh, so to speak."

"No, no lad, that's Mavis the little Madam, you might say. She comes down here every Friday night. Same routine. Sneaks in the door when no one's looking, stands there for a bit looking all *'come on then lads'*. Gets noticed then goes out without any trouble when Walter the barman clocks her."

"Why does she do that then?"

"Well son, she is what is known as *'a lady of the night'*. She comes in to let the men know she's around, tempts them with her little wiggling charade we've just seen, goes back out again, round to the alley, to the side door - the door that all the men have to go through to get to the toilets. So, if anyone fancies a bit of, you know, kiss and cuddle, she's in the alley where it's dark and hard to see. So, if you see a sudden stream of men all heading for the door saying 'Toilets', mark my words, it is more than one type of relief they are looking for."

"What do you mean? Why does she do that? Hasn't she got a feller of her own? I would have thought a cracking looking girl like that would have no trouble finding one."

"No, you daft twit. She charges men money. Any man. As many men as possible, for having sex with her."

I went red with the blush of all blushes. Dad said the word *'sex'*. I didn't know where to look or what to say. I'd never heard me dad talk about stuff like that before. I had never heard any grownup for that matter. Even the lads at school didn't say that much about, you know, not really; it was all a bit hush-hush. Just a wink and a nod when something a bit saucy was suggested. But that was it, I thought. I found out later I had led a sheltered life.

I knew how it made me feel though, seeing women looking all attractive like, but I never knew what to do about it. I had never been up close. I mean I was only sixteen and you weren't supposed to be doing stuff, I mean thinking of lasses like that anyway not till you were married. Nearest I ever got to a lass was a few months back when I called round for Chalkie. Elena came to the door. I saw her standing behind her mum in the doorway, pretending she wasn't looking. Not like that night outside the pub when she looked at me with those eyes. I know she did. But it was hard trying to catch her eye with her mum standing right in front of me. I used to dream about her nights since then. I could see her face with her shining eyes and her pink cheeks all soft like. She had a smile, she had lips and a neck. Made me quiver she did. I'd noticed that in the last wee while. I'd begin to quiver when I thought about kissing her. Then I'd get all embarrassed and have to force mesel to stop thinking. Don't be daft Rob, I would say. She wouldn't want you doing that. Elena was like a filmstar to me, pure, perfect high up there, Mmmm. I must stop daydreaming.

I could tell me dad had cottoned on that I was a bit embarrassed. I knew that men and women were made different an' that but, well, but that's it. The rest was just guesswork. On the rare times I'd thought about it, I figured, when the time comes, instinct will take over. I know you are supposed to be married before you can, well, you know...do stuff together.

"We'll need to have a chat sometime soon," me dad said.

*Thank God!* For a minute there, I thought he was going to start right there and then, in the middle of the pub, with everyone and anyone nebbin' in.

Chalkie was smirkin' under his tilted head, watching me squiggle, enjoying my embarrassment, pretending he wasn't embarrassed himself, suddenly all big brother, like. Wink, wink. That was something for him. The beer must have loosened him up too.

# 12. Sergeant Mayhew's Secret

Thankfully, the heavy footsteps of the local bobby approaching through the pub doors broke the tension. His head was held high with his helmet tightly fastened under his chin. Carrying an air of authority and wearing a smug look, he took six steps up to the bar like he was counting them. He nodded to Elsie the barmaid and our Walter with a pleasant but official greeting.

"Good evening, all. How are things tonight? Everything alright? No trouble I hope."

"All's well tonight, Sarg, all quiet on the western front as they say!

It was ten minutes to ten.

Walter called out across the room, "Last orders, gentlemen, please! Last orders now!"

Apparently, this happened every night. Closing time for the pub was 10 'o'clock. The barman called last orders at ten minutes before closing time and everybody had till exactly ten o'clock on the dot to get their orders in and ten minutes after that to the minute, to get the last drink down.

And every Friday night, it seemed, at twelve minutes to ten, Sergeant Mayhew entered the pub and went through the same routine me dad said. After Walter put the towels across the beer pumps and rang the bell telling the men to drink up, at exactly ten o'clock Sergeant Mayhew would turn and go on his merry way.

*He's a bit smug and superior.* I thought to mesel.

"I suppose he has his job to do," I said out loud.

"Oh no," me dad said. "He didn't have a smug look on his face for nothing you, know."

"What do you mean?" I asked.

"Mavis, that lass in the red, the lady of the night. We found out recently, just before she comes in of a Friday night, in order to make sure she doesn't get nicked for prostitution, our fine Sergeant here gets a free session with her up the other end of the alley. One of the men caught them at it one night. After chatting about it we all decided not to let on. That kind of information might come in handy some time or other, you never know."

"What, that lovely lass that was just in, with the high heels and the legs? She's kissin' and cuddlin' with Sergeant Mayhew, that old man? But he's older than you dad, isn't he?" Surprising myself talking like that.

"Well, lad, that is the wicked way of the wicked world of wicked men, and women of course. Be warned and stay away. Wait till you find yourself a decent lass and get married and settled down. That's the right way to do things. Wait and do it proper and legal like. If you get caught with the likes of young Mavis, you'll end up in clink and probably with the clap into the bargain. And I don't mean applause neither."

"What's the clap, Dad?"

"Never you mind that for now. You don't want it anyways. Let me assure you of that. Many a poor lad has fallen prey to her charms and lived to regret it for a very long and painful time afterwards. Someday, when you are older, I'll tell you more about it."

"But Dad! I thought I was a man now. Isn't that what tonight's all about?" I says.

"Well, yes, you are kind of but not fully, not yet son. Wait till yer eighteen. I'll talk to you about it then."

# 13. Time for Home

I couldn't believe four hours had passed so quickly and it was time to go home. With all that had gone on we hadn't noticed the time slipping by.

Walter the barman shouted out again above all the chatter, clanging his irritating brass bell. "Drink up now! Let's have yer glasses, men! Time to go home to your beloved trouble-and-strife and your cuddly bundles of joy."

There weren't any women or children in the public bar. They usually only got to go into the snug, a tiny room just off the street with a sliding hatch through to the bar and a wooden bench to the side, just big enough for two not-too-stout women. Any others who wanted to come in had to stand. Sometimes women would go into the lounge, the posher bit, but only if they were with their men.

Dad nudged me and Chalkie. "Come on lads. Drink up. I guess we had better get back now and face the music."

It wasn't till I stood up that I realised that I was probably drunk. My head began to spin, and I staggered some as I headed for the door. Chalkie was just ahead of me. He didn't look any better.

"Ooh, steady boy!" I said as I reached out to grasp his arm to steady meself and slow him down a bit.

We bundled through the swing doors together. Dad said cheerio to his mates behind us. "Safe journey home lads?" Then came a spontaneous rendition of Vera Lynne's, *'We'll meet again, don't know where, don't know when,'* as the three of us broke tunelessly and loudly into what barely passed for singing.

Drunk?

Maybe.

Paralytic?

No, not really.

Seriously well oiled?

Definitely.

We walked back home with Chalkie as far as the corner where I had picked him up on the way in. No one spoke for a bit. There was a kind of a hush in the cold night air. It was October. The nights had pulled in and it was dark. The sky was clear, the stars were twinkling, sparkly, happy pinpricks of light in an otherwise dreary world. For a few seconds, it transfixed me, anchored my gaze upwards towards the heavens as we shuffled and staggered together, swaying the unchoreographed dance of half-drunk fools. I stifled the temptation to sing.

As I looked up into the night sky, I turned my face to let it bathe in the light of the moon. An overwhelming sense of joy coursed through me as my eyes drank in the panoramic view of the incredible universe. And it wasn't the beer. In fact, it was an oddly sobering sense of joy. It was a sensation even better than the feeling the beer gave me.

It was free and healthy, full of life.

But it didn't last.

Like vapour, it slipped away leaving only the faint hint of its visit.

But its memory stayed with me.

In later life, as I reflected back, I asked myself why I hadn't taken hold of that moment more firmly, why hadn't I paid more attention to that magical glimpse of that other world, the one beyond this one. Why didn't I investigate it more, pursue it, find out where it came from, who made it and why. Things could have been so different. Looking back, I realised in that fleeting moment of awareness was a message from someone beyond the visible seeking to catch my attention, calling out to me there was more, more than what I was seeing while hurtling through life, shoulders hunched, eyes pressed downwards, gawpin' at the earth, distracted by its sorrows and fleeting pleasures.

*'There is more to life than this, Rob me lad!'* The silent voice from the heavens seemed to whisper just then for a few fleeting seconds.

Back on our Smoggie planet (*'Smoggies' is* what folks from Middlesborough were known as), a quite different voice brought me down to *terra firma.*

"See yer tomorrow, Rob," Chalkie slurred, as we reached the corner, the parting of the ways so to speak.

"Mind how you go," dad responded. "Have you got a key? Mind those milk bottles in the alley. You don't want to wake the old yins up in your state."

"What do you mean 'in my state'? I'm perfectly alright thank you very much." Chalkie, in his defiant and youthful pride defended, slurring his speech.

There was a fish'n'chip shop with an open doorway on the corner of the building next to where we stood. The smell was brilliant. Fernando was busy with a handful of customers but like most of the folks round here took the time to say hi, "Hi Tom, hi lads, you all okay there?" Dad answered for us all, "Proper champion thanks Fernando—see yer busy again."

"Fancy a bag of chips before you go?" I asked Chalkie.

"I do. I do. I do. Mate. But I'd better get back."

"As had we, son," my dad broke in, putting his hand on my shoulder. "Your mother won't be best pleased anyway, us being so late already and that."

A different kind of chill came over us both.

"Okay, Chalkie," I half whispered, as if afraid of being discovered. "Okay, mate. See you later. Sunday maybe?"

Chalkie headed off on his last few hundred yards. We turned the corner of Cannon Street, headed on up to the far end of Denmark Street for home.

# 14. War Zone No 2

We reached our front door minutes later. "Let's go round the back," Dad said. "We won't make so much noise." Down the alley we went, quietly entering through the side door, hoping it didn't squeak and that mother had gone to bed. We passed through the back kitchen into the hallway. There was light under the door.

"Flippin 'eck!" Dad said. "We're for it now. She's still up."

He opened the living room door.

Mother screeched at us the minute we stepped into the room.

"Where the bloody hell do you think you two have been till this time of night? I've been sitting here on me own in front of this excuse for a fire waiting for ages. We've hardly any coal left, or had you forgotten? You were going to fetch some tonight from the yard, weren't you? And it's Rob's birthday, or have you bloody well forgotten that as well? I got a cake and some sandwiches ready." She was half screaming at us.

As we edged further into the room, it became obvious to her where we'd been all evening. Not that she didn't know already.

"You've been down that bloody pub again, haven't you? Doesn't take a genius to work that one out. You couldn't wait to get him into your drunken ways, could you?"

She was red-faced now. She was a small woman but portly - not quite rotund but heading that way. She liked to bake. She liked cakes, especially Madeira sponge with jam filling and butter cream icing.

"No! I haven't forgot. That's why we are late. Yes, I took him down the pub. We always go down the pub Fridays. You know that. And he's sixteen now. He's allowed to drink. I didn't know you were going to put on a spread, did I?"

"You never bloody well bothered to ask," she retorted. "You just go off in the morning without a word and I'm supposed to guess what you have in mind, am I?"

"Well I've had enough of this carry on, leavin' me alone all day and night wi' nowt in me purse and nowt in the pantry while you are off enjoyin' yourself, drinking the rent and bloody housekeeping no doubt. I've had enough of it."

She had worked herself up to full rage by then. She reached down into the fireplace and picked up the poker. She stood up, straight-backed, head back and leathered into me dad, just about cracking his skull open. I was terrified. He put his arms up to defend himself. She caught him a glancing blow, skimming his forehead and a thin trickle of blood began to stream down his face. He staggered backwards, landin' on the arm of the sofa before topplin' backwards onto it.

I didn't know what to do. "No mam!" I called out. "Don't! Don't hit me dad like that! You'll kill him! It's not his fault. I wanted to go. Look he's bleeding, leave him alone. It's supposed to be me birthday."

I moved to grab her arm. She turned to face me, her fierceness unabated, arm still in the air, she gave me a look as sore as any blow. She meant business alright.

I stepped back, "You go to your room an get yerself off to bed if you know what's good for you or you'll get a leatherin' as well, birthday or no bloody birthday!"

When mother got into a rage there was no reasoning wi' her. It happened often. Not usually with me around. And as far as I knew, not usually with the poker in her hand either. I often heard them when I was in bed. They argued and argued. She shoutin' and screaming at him. He didn't say much a lot of the time, just every now and again when he thought she had gone too far, he would chip in with some frustrated self-defence, helpless really to know what to do with her. It was always about money or the pub or him not doin' anything around the house, or her being left on her own, or only having one kid, and what kind of a man did he think he was? I would hide under the bedclothes, anxious, terrified really. No idea what to do. I just wanted it to stop, for them to get on wi' each other, do things together, enjoy life. Why couldn't they love each other and be nice for a change? I didn't know many older folks who did seem to love each other. Everybody seemed to be at each other's throats all the time. Except when they'd had a few.

I would read books to take me mind off things, but I could only do that in the summer if it were still light. In the winter when it got dark nights early, I had to pinch the torch from the coal shed to read under the covers. Me mam said we couldn't afford to keep the lights on all the time. So, I'd read books for a bit by torchlight, or else I would daydream about my comics or stories. She always seemed to know when I had taken the torch, cos the batteries ran down that quick. Sometimes I would think about Elena, Chalkie's now not-so-little sister. She seemed to have grown more and more into something special. She was somewhere nice to take my mind to. She was gentle, kind-natured, she'd got a good heart. You could tell. We hadn't talked much since she left school and started nursing, but I thought of her a lot still.

It's funny how much you can sense from a person's face. She would just stand in the doorway of her house looking over her mam's shoulder, smiling. There was something going on there with me and her, I think she knew it too.

Anyway that night, I went to my room without further argument. I got into bed and covered my head with the candlewick bedspread and put my hands over my ears trying not to hear. I squeezed my eyes tight shut to block out the strobe like haunting images of mam's swinging arm landing on me dad's head. Images that kept flashing through my mind. That poker, that moment it bounced off that fragile place on my dad's head, that image repeated itself over and over, when it struck him, it struck terror into me.

All the emotions, the muscles, even the bones of my thin body shook and shook till I was worn out. Fear had taken a hold of me. Like someone threw a switch in my brain. I couldn't find it to switch it off. I was already an anxious kid. But that fear pressed my terror buttons harder and harder. It's burning fiery flare followed me through life like Gollum in Lord of the Rings, a spiteful unwanted fiend. Fear was my fiercest enemy, the cause of my undoing, all but.

Decades later, I *'stumbled across'* the great fire extinguisher of fear, a more powerful force than all those blazes of hell. I encountered the key; I located the switch that turned off fear and turned on the flow of inner peace.

But just there, then the full force of fear faced me down and it felt like it was winning.

# 15. In the Middle of the Night

Eventually I fell into a fitful sleep, half waking, hearing the clanking of pots in the kitchen, doors slamming, occasional outbursts, mostly from my mother mumbling to herself. I guessed dad was okay, although he had looked pretty bad when I turned in.

I woke up in the middle of the night around two o'clock, bursting for a pee. The house was quiet and dark. The toilet was outside in a shed at the end of the garden. Two other families shared it from the same row of houses.

I fetched the lamp from the coal shed just outside the back door. I could see my way up the earthen path okay. I put my hand out and opened the toilet door. I got the fright of my life. Dad was in there sitting slumped forward on the toilet. I thought for a minute he was dead. But no, thank God, he had just fallen asleep. My opening the door must have startled him. He flung his arms up in the air in a waking frenzy to defend himself.

"Who's that?" he called out. "What's going on?"

"It's only me, Dad. Just me. Are you all right? What are you doing out here? You looked as if you were dead! I got a right shocker."

Small smudges of dried blood were crusted on his heavy, wrinkled forehead.

"Dad, I don't want to be a pain but I'm bustin' for a pee."

"Okay, lad, okay," he groaned as he struggled to his feet. He staggered a bit as he made his way into the garden. I watched him as he stopped by the shed and lit himself a Woodbine. I rushed into the toilet, snapped the door closed, only just remembering to lift the toilet seat. People gave yer what for if you didn't. I was that desperate I didn't care, but force of habit had kicked in and saved me a clip round the ear. I don't think grownups could help themselves doing that. You would get a thump round the lug for just lookin' the wrong way.

It was a right smelly hole that toilet—chemicals and, well, you know. I was desperate to get in and just as glad to get out. Dad was still in the backyard with his fag.

"Are you coming inside now, Dad?"

"Aye, I'll be right in, son. I'll get me head down for a few hours and see if I can get out before your ma gets up. I promised your Aunty Beryl I'd go up the old railway line with her lad and get some wood and coal for her as well. Her Larry's sick you know and that young lad of theirs ...Ian, 'es not up to much when it comes to work. One of these dreamers you know, likes books and airy-fairy poetry. His head's in the clouds most of the time. Not like you, lad. You know what hard work is even at your age. I'll get me head down on the sofa, son. It's a bit short for me but better than sleepin' on the cold lino. You get off to bed."

"No, dad." I said, "Why don't you sleep in my bed? I can  better sleep on the sofa. I'm not as tall as you. Go on. I don't mind."

"Okay, lad. Thanks son. You can come with us tomorrow if you like, but you'll have to be up and about by seven. Your mother likes to lay in at the weekend, so she'll not rouse much before nine, an' if she's still in a mood, even later. We can get a mug o' tea and a slice of toast at your Aunt Beryl's. She said she'd see us right for grub if we help her out."

Off to our different beds we went. Next morning came fast and hard. I didn't know how dad was, but all that drinking had got me fuzzy brained. My head was thick. Waking up was a struggle.

# 16. Saturday Morning

We managed to leave the house safely and in good time. We spent the morning looking for wood and coal up the old railway line. Larry's lad, Ian, came with us. Aunty Beryl gave us some tea and toast and a little pack of sandwiches and a bottle of water to take with us. Nobody had much of anything, but folks round our way would share what they had.

It was good to be out in the country under the fresh October skies, in the cool morning sharpness and the stubbled fields, far away from the aggro and fighting at home, away from the hard slog in the factory and the smog of the killing air we breathed all week. The morning flew by as we combed our way through the rugged countryside, chit chatting, commenting on the bird songs, the autumn colours, the various hues of the sky, and the smell of the remaining harvest being brought in, a bit late that year. We picked a few brambles along the railway siding. They looked like they were starving too - a bit scrawny this year.

"There hasn't been enough rain," me dad said.

Ian trudged along behind us occasionally joining in. As me dad said, his head was stuck in a tattered poetry book he'd brought with him. Every now and then he read something out loud until we got fed up and would tell him to shut it and do something useful with his life.

"Poetry is for fairies and toffs!" me dad said.

Ian clammed up till we stopped for elevenses at half past ten.

We stopped and sat down on the edge of a harvested field, found a bit of left-over straw to sit on and settled ourselves down for a rest. Me dad took off his flat cap which he wore everywhere. Nearly all the men in Yorkshire did, least round our way. It became the County emblem practically, especially when the newspaper started the daily Andy Capp Cartoon series.

He leaned back on his elbow and gazed out across the curve of the land. The autumn-coloured trees stood like guardians in the distance along the edge of the field. The air was clear and the sky a pale aqua blue with thin stretched muslin clouds in water-colour patches in an artists' sky. Ian lay on his belly leaning on his two elbows, his head stuck even deeper into his book. I sat upright, legs crossed in front of me. We were hungry; scavenging was hard work. We tucked into the little feast Aunt Beryl had given us, gobbling the few small sandwiches of fish paste, washing it down with our bottle of Yorkshire

Moors (straight-from-the-tap) water. "Tap juice" we called it.

Not turning his head, me dad called to Ian.

"Read us that poem, that one about Autumn you started on earlier. Read us a bit of that again."

Ian was as surprised as I was but happily obliged. You could tell Ian had something. He didn't just read the words. He felt them. They came alive in him. Autumn came alive too as we heard him read out loud a few verses.

This is a poem written by a man called John Keats, he starts out, it's called....

## To Autumn

*'Season of mists and mellow fruitfulness,*

*close bosom-friend of the maturing sun;*

*conspiring with him how to load and bless*

*with fruit the vines that round the thatch-eves run; to*

*bend with apples the moss'd cottage-trees, and fill all*

*fruit with ripeness to the core;*

*to swell the gourd, and plump the hazel shells*

*with a sweet kernel; to set budding more,*

*and still more, later flowers for the bees,*

*until they think warm days will never cease,*

*for Summer has o'er-brimm'd their clammy cells.*

When he finished, Ian said,

"Poetry is not just for fairies and toffs, Mr Fentiman. It's for thoughtful minds, for hearts that feel, and worn-out souls. For people like us. Ordinary people, young and old. Poetry takes you to a place far away, out of the troubles of this world. It's funny, but it kind of heals you, you know. And it's not just for the upper classes or the rich. We might be just working-class people but we're not all thick or stupid. We read great books. We love good music. We invent great things. We appreciate anything beautiful, maybe more than others who are better off, cleverer, or higher up in society.

Life covers our souls with so much hardship and ugliness, those things which are beautiful come to us as a kind of healing; whether its poetry, good literature, music, drama, nature, whatever is good and beautiful. Truly beautiful things are *'a threshold to the divine, a step away from heaven's door.'* Well, so one of my favourite writers says."

Ian paused and then went on to say.

"I don't know if you ever read the Good Book, Mr Fentiman, but there is a bit in there where Jesus says to a great crowd of people sitting out on a hillside - a bit like us right now - he says, 'Blessed are you poor, for yours is the Kingdom of Heaven.' Now we all believe Heaven is the most glorious place there is, full of unimaginable beauty and perfection. And Jesus is saying—that's for us, that beauty, and that perfection, for us poor ones, beautiful things Mr Fentiman for me and for thee."

A bit flummoxed, taken aback by Ian's words,

"I don't know about all that, young Ian," Dad says, but then concedes, "You're obviously not as daft as you seem, lad." He delivered the words in his usual blunt Yorkshire manner.

"But listening to what you read just now did me good son. Thanks. It did my old heart good, right enough."

Then he pulled himself back to his own world image of his own Yorkshire dyed in the wool self.

"Meantime lads, we've got to live in the here-and-now on planet earth. Let's get back to collecting coal for Aunt Beryl. We've got a bit to do yet. And we need to be back home for one o'clock and get cleaned up. It's the Miners Brass Band do down at the Bandstand at 2 o'clock this afternoon."

I was just about to ask what time it was when the church bell peeled out its solemn soul-searching ring eleven times, reassuring us that all was well. God was still up there in his heavens, and earth was still spinning on its steady-as-she-goes axis.

Called to our feet, now planted squarely and firmly on *terra firma* by dad's practical prompting, we cracked on with the rummaging, the grubbing along the sidings to root out fallen scraps of coal or wood to make Aunt Beryl's and our existence a bit cosier, if nothing else.

Dog tired, we returned to Auntie Beryl's in good time, loaded some of the wood and coal into the shed and headed back home with the rest to get some grub and to get ready for the concert, unsure of what reception we would get from mother.

Mother was out. She left no note with her usual list of instructions. But dinner was plated up in the oven. We were still getting fed. That was something.

After eating together in silence at the kitchen table, dad sat reading his newspaper and listening to the radio. I went off to my room. I was reading a book I borrowed from the library, *The Man in the Iron Mask*. The story gripped me and kept me from nodding off.

Just as well. I got a big enough shock when Dad banged on the bedroom door, "Come on, lad. It's time to go. Get cleaned up. We'll need to head off in about ten minutes."

"Isn't Mother coming with us?"

"No idea where she is, son. We'll head off anyway. Maybe she'll come along with your Aunty Joan. She sometimes visits her on a Saturday."

# 17. The Bandstand

Starbank Park was crowded that day. Formerly open fields, the park was designed for walking and enjoying the scenery, developed in Victorian times in response to a growing concern for health and wellbeing. As music was seen to influence moral health, bandstands became focal points for community entertainment. The sunshine and the clear autumn sky drew the multitudes outdoors.

At the heart of it all, the Brass Band was the real attraction. Nothing expressed the Yorkshire community spirit better. Music born, bred, and blown through a Yorkshireman's trumpet, French horn, trombone, tuba, or euphonium united Yorkshire people like nothing else. Ian would say there's something spiritual about it too.

*"Music is divine",* I could hear him say. *"Young or old, poor or better off, daft or clever, man, woman or child, it casts its magic spell over all without judgement or favour. It helps people forget their troubles, their petty and not so petty squabbles, helps cheer up their otherwise cheerless lives. It brings people together."*

The crowds flocked to the park. People lived back then in a swirl of differing emotions about things that affected everyone's lives. Some felt the relief and almost joyfulness of believing the headlines of recent months that the Great Depression was behind them, letting loose a desire to celebrate, as if to grab tight hold of the hope that gave them. Others were flattened by the competing prospect of another war ahead, giving understandable cause for fearfulness and gloom.

These all too rare concerts were a kind of celebration of life, declaring victory over adversity. Community Brass Band music was a healer. It soothed troubled minds and hearts and helped push away the fears. Community concerts were part of the glue that helped bind us together.

Whatever individual musical tastes were, all types came to these events.

They drew everyone in, even the ones who complained the music wasn't as good as it was in the old days, and the ones who preferred the modern big-band sounds of Glen Miller or Artie Shaw. Concert Day was Concert Day, that old familiar Brass Band Day. Tradition rooted men, women, and children alike in the solid foundation of what was truly Yorkshire, the product of a thousand years of history.

An air of conviviality swirled around the ornate bandstand in the centre of the park. Wide stretches of lush green grass were dotted around with maple, ash, oak, and beech trees. Secluded and open areas alike offered wooden benches inviting folks to rest awhile and enjoy the scenery. The occasional vendor sold ice cream or donuts, hot tea, or Bovril to folks from Guisborough and South Shields, but mostly from nearby.

Set on an island, the octagonal, cast-iron bandstand was visible from any angle. Designed with striking and intricate features, one of many up and down the country, the bandstand was set apart on the edge of a small inland lake dressed with weeping willows and embraced at the edges by clumps of water reeds and bulrushes like a scarf around the shoulders. The water itself was adorned with large-leafed water lilies fit for any princely frog. The delicate pink and red flowers at their centre had their petals pointing upwards, cupped as though catching dew from heaven, or maybe gathering up the hidden tears from our crestfallen souls. The imagination could run wildly riot with such vivid scenes of nature's best.

It was still bright daylight and there was a faint smell of wild mushrooms. The birds had gone early to bed settled in their trees, ready to listen. The laughter of children and the happy chatter of men and women filled the vacuum of nature's early rest. If the mind's eye could look down upon the scene from above, upon a landscape resembling one of Constable's country paintings, it would have seen the gentle, swirling movement of the crowds as they weaved their way to their chosen spot. It would have seen the beauty of a people enjoying harmony with its own known world, with nature, and with music.

There was a glistening of the sun on the tilting brass instruments. Eyes were drawn to the musicians in the bandstand as they began to tune up for the concert.

Dad and I walked briskly through the big black iron gates, followed by Ian and Aunt Beryl who were trotting in our wake. Not far in, I spied Chalkie with Elena and their mum ahead of us. Thank God their grumpy old dad wasn't there. They were walking towards our mam and our Aunt Joan who were sitting on a bench a good bit further up near the tea wagon and not far from the bandstand. *This should be fun,* I thought. I could see Dad wince as he spotted them. Straightening himself up, he braced himself for an earbashing. You never knew with mother how she would be on any given day, or in any given situation. We made a beeline for the crowd of them. Nothing else for it. To avoid them would only store up wrath and blue murder for when we got home.

Mother was a domineering character. She was also chalk and cheese. Indoors she could be a monster, but when out in company she would be jovial, chatty, the life and soul. Indoors, the sugar and spice element must have been used up years ago, but outdoors, well, it was the face of all things nice to the world. Having said that, she had an ego as huge as a small mountain and there was no room for another ego in her company. If it came to a clash, you'd better read the signs if you didn't want public and fierce humiliation. She could slice a soul in two, faster than a cut throat razor.

Mother needed the company. That was her food for life, her meat, the nourishment she craved for feeding her self-esteem. If she could attract and keep everyone's attention, speak over everyone and anyone without a care, or a hint of fear, all the while wearing a polite, shallow, I-really-am-superior smile, she could bask in her sense of self-importance for another while. Inwardly she was deeply sad, deeply disappointed, deeply resentful that life had not lived up to her high expectations of wealth, status, and popularity. It was therefore strange to stand listening to her holding rapturous court with everyone out here on this glorious day. It was hard not to think of her last night fiercely frowning under her dark cloud of madness, almost murdering dad with her rage, her violent tongue, and ready fist. My emotions cascaded down a man-sized tunnel of confusion. She was my mother, the giver of my life, the woman wife of my gentle if not sometimes gruff dad, the bosom source of life and female love, yet also the excruciating demon of my fear ridden body. She was some other person, a stranger, even an enemy but a friend too all at once.

It was strange too to look there at her, and then in a short turn of the head, look over at Elena. Elena, my dream with the flashing eyes, Chalkie's lovely, fresh, young, sister standing just a few feet away from me, tantalizingly attractive to my young desperate heart. What a contrast.

Elena was dressed in a light blue frock that hung beneath her knees under her warm-looking duffle coat. I could see her white ankle socks and black shoes with a clasp-over silver buckle. She had on a woollen hat resting on wavy auburn locks that captivate me, always. I stood gazing at her, oblivious to the crowds and thinking. She had a red scarf wrapped around her slim white neck. Her face was soft and bright. She had eyes and honest lips, rosy cheeks and small, intriguing ears. She carried adventure in a gentle spirit. I watched her interact with people. When she spoke, she also listened. She was genuinely interest in people. You could feel her warmth without touching her. Maybe I idealised her, what with me desperate for something lovely to fill my sad emptiness. I remembered Ian's favourite author who said, *"Beauty is the threshold to the divine."*

Elena was beauty to me. She was divine.

I contrasted all these thoughts with my mother.

I asked myself again, *'How did this happen? Was mother like this once too? Was she? Could she have been? What happened to make her like she is now?'*

Talk about beauty and the beast. Sorry Mum, but we are Yorkshire after all. A spade's a spade.

That afternoon, outside the house, in public, in the park, at the bandstand, mother was smiling, engaging with everyone and anyone in high octane conversation, about anything and everything and nothing very much at all. Trying to follow a conversation with this group was like trying to unravel cooked spaghetti one strand at a time. So many words, so many topics, interwoven, jumping from one thing to another then back again. What was it all about? What did it all mean? What was the point of it all?

# 18. Let the Music Begin

As we gathered around the park bench where mother and Aunt Joan were sitting, the banter flew back and forth between us all.

Except me and Dad.

We stood on the fringes and kept smiling attentively, praying there would be no public outburst.

You never knew.

Us young ones - Chalkie, Ian, Elena, and me - were included but not really expected to say anything useful or sensible. We knew we were to speak when spoken to, and not before, just smile and be polite.

The band stirred and the music began to play, we looked around at the musicians. Following the conductors lead, the players raised their golden instruments and on the Maestro's cue they began to play the Finale to Rossini's William Tell Overture. They blew out all its fullness and rousing pomp filling the park air with life, the notes dancing and darting through the trees, their sounds skippelling across the pond, caressing the lush green grass and it stopped, finishing abruptly, as it should. A few seconds passed in silence, then thunderous applause and rapturous cheers.

My dad spoke first.

"Marvellous, my, that was grand. They didn't miss a beat and they were travelling at breakneck speed. What a performance!"

Others joined in with the beaming enthusiasm of a transformed people. *'Tremendous.' 'The best of Yorkshire.' 'Never heard anything like it.' 'Absolutely bloody marvellous.' 'Those drummers!' 'Them cornet players, incredible.'*

Minutes later when the crowd settled down, there was a change of mood as the band played Elgar's Nimrod. Many of us didn't know the actual titles of the music, but we saw the names printed on leaflets that had been scattered around the place.

"Terrific!" I heard one man say. "I don't care what anybody thinks, that music expressed all that is good about Great Britain. And yes, I say again, Great Britain. I don't care what people say about racism, national pride is different, something to be cherished and honoured. We should be proud of all the good and despise the bad. We can always change in the future. That's what I say."

Another man, just behind us chipped into the conversation. "Anyone who doesn't see the good in this must have been dropped on their heads as bairns. Maybe someone should do it again."

"Now, now, come on," the first man retorted. "It's a free country. Folks are entitled to their opinion." He added, half laughing, "even if they are wrong."

The band played on, and the banter and bravado rose higher and louder as the intervals allowed. Around halfway through, a small army of youngsters went round with empty cocoa tins to take up a collection on behalf of the charity the band were supporting. Folks didn't have much, but they gave what they could - many a widow's mite falling to the bottom of the tins that day.

After the break, a few announcements were made by the band leader and then the twenty-two musicians started up again enthralling us all with many favourites like the Lucerne Song and the Dance of the Tumblers, finishing with Rule Britannia and Land of Hope and Glory, followed by even more rapturous applause. If cheering could win a war, then we would have had nowt to fear.

'Eeeeee by gum! That was proper champion, that was!" blurted a red-faced old man with a pendulous belly and a grin that could have disarmed the Devil himself.

'If there is a God," another man said, "He'd be a brass band man wi' a whippet, a flat cap, live in

Yorkshire, sup ale, eat fish' n' chips and serve communion in a Yorkshire pudding."

Mother, not to be outdone offered her bit too. "Aye, we might talk a bit queer as folks say, and we might seem a bit daft, but there's not much we can't do up here in Yorkshire when it comes to brass bands. We have the best. Second to none."

"Who couldn't smile listening to this!" Aunt Joan's voice was barely heard beneath life's commanding oracle on all things.

"Absolutely fabulous!" Elena voiced looking up, her swan like neck stretching upwards to the heavens breathing quietly into the air, not caring who or what or if anyone heard.

Even Chalkie was mesmerised by the stirring performance. "That was phenomenal!" he actually said out loud. I could hardly believe my ears, Chalkie getting enthusiastic, and it wasn't football he was talking about.

Ian of course had something semi-profound to say. He couldn't help himself. He quoted from the great bard.

*If music be the food of love, play on;*
*give me excess of it, that, surfeiting,*
*the appetite may sicken, and so die.*
*That strain again! It had a dying fall:*

*O, it came o'er my ear like the sweet sound,*
*that breathes upon a bank of violets,*
"If music be the food of love, play on…" He repeated.

"Alright, Ian. Thanks very much, son," me dad said. "I think the great bard's romantic finery is lost here today. This is Yorkshire, son. We're all brass bands and down to earth here. We're not high-faluting romancers."

"Let him alone," Mother sniped. "Not everyone is as uneducated and hard-hearted as you men."

She spats the words out like a cobra.

"What? I didn't believe I was hearing right" I looked at me dad. I could imagine his inner scream. *'Who the bloody hell does she think she is then, us men hard hearted. What?'*

I was poised tense to hear his response.

It seemed the wisdom of years lead him to move quickly away, he turned, face fixed like flint, with thoughts unspoken. He headed out towards the gate. His reaction was abrupt, noticeable, but the safer option. We were not unfazed by mother's habit of cutting people down. Fortunately we were still high on the ecstasy, the blissful anaesthetic of the multitudinous emotions, the pride, nostalgia, sorrow, love, hope, and gladness that the music had awakened in us.

We headed home in quiet disorganised procession, like silent ants all knowing our place, where we were going, what we had to do, no need to talk, mesmerised by joy.

The brass band had stirred up all sorts of reflection in our souls.

It wasn't religion, but it was not without it's reverence.

We were heading for home, but if home was truly where the heart is, my heart was still with natures expansive beauty in the park, the music and maybe just a little bit of me with Elena. That was the home of my heart just then. But it was Saturday evening, and it was time to go back to the house where we lived.

Saturday nights were often spent reading the newspaper, listening to armchair theatre on the radio and with mother sometimes preparing food for Sunday or baking her favourite Madeira sponge. The nine o'clock news from the BBC signalled when it was nearing time for bed.

Even though Friday night had seen such a violent outburst, that Saturday night passed with a reasonable level of normality. Order and disciplined routine were maintained as far as possible, even after times when chaos had broken out. Nothing ever really got sorted out, talked about, properly discussed, let alone resolved. Carry on as if nothing had happened seemed to be the strategy for a peaceful life.

I went to bed at nine fifteen after the news. I had my book and the secretly borrowed torch to use under the bedclothes. The air was silent on the surface, but angry blue underneath.

"Goodnight, mam. Goodnight, dad. Sleep well."

"You too son," dad responded. Mother was silent, except for a short grunt.

Maybe she was already asleep in her armchair.

Being angry all the time must have been very tiring.

# 19. Sunday Morning

Sunday started like a silent movie. Mam and dad were sat in the living room when I got up. They were not talking, not unusual. The atmosphere was charged with supressed emotion.

They sat leaden and still like dead people. They filled the armchairs either side of the smoky coal fire flickering, struggling to survive, just like their relationship. Although there were no words, the stillness transmitted tangible, almost audible, waves of anger. Their pain and misery were screaming out to be heard, to be healed, to be touched with some hoped for tenderness. *Where had their lost love gone?* I sat in the living room, on the chair by the front window looking out onto the main street. It was ten o'clock in the morning. No one in our house rose early on Sundays.

The sky outside was overcast but dry and the overnight wind had died down. There was a strange calm in the street, drawing me out of the house, out of the mental misery that was sucking me into its gloom indoors. As I looked out the window across the road the street was busy enough; people sitting in their open doorways, men reading papers, kids playing quietly, wives with mugs of tea blethering to each other in muted voices, that was the usual scene on a Sunday morning. People walked by on both sides, some dressed up in their Sunday best, heading for church, I guessed. Even poor people tried to smarten up on Sundays.

We never went to church, not usually, 'cept for funerals, or christenings. We went at Christmas and Easter, did our duty.

"We have to," me dad would say. "Everybody is expected to go, else folks think somat is wrong wi yer."

I wondered if I should go along on me own some Sunday, especially when there was nowt on, and the house was like it was today. I didn't know if they would let me in without me mam or dad. Most of the lads I knew only went if their parents took them along. Dad maybe would have gone, maybe, but mother never. "A right bunch of hypocrites," she would say.

"All fur coats and no knickers. Busy-body, do-goody nosey parkers. They only go for the gossip and the free tea and biscuits, to make themselves feel better about their pathetic lives. It's their weekly injection of delusion. Like morphine, something to relieve the pain of living and breathing all day. People like to believe pie-in-the-sky fairy stories about a make-believe Santa Claus. It's just their insurance policy for the afterlife. Doesn't make a damn bit of difference to how they live down here, just as much cussin' and swearing, carrying on and hanky-panky goes on wi them as the rest of us."

Mum preferred her Magic Circle, or whatever that spooky stuff was called that she got up to with her sisters.

"I think I'll go round to see how Chalkie is," I said.

Not a word of response. I stood up. Dad lifted his head in recognition, sent a faint grin my way, then his head went right back down again... silently.

"I'm off out," I said, once I was in the hall. I said it into the air, not expecting any response. No response came. I headed out anyway.

Mother's restraint relented. "Don't you be late back home," she called out as I was about to open the front door. "Your tea will be ready at six. Make sure you're on time or the dog next door will be getting it."

The neighbour kept whippets.

"Okay, Ma. See you at six."

"I'll be off out at half six to your Auntie Nora's tonight," she shouted. "It's our night for the cards." I knew she was referring to the Tarots. "We'll maybe do the boards as well and see if we can get a message for you and me to get us out of this bloody hellhole."

There she was cosying up to me just to get at me dad and trying to get me onside.

I tensed up. Everything in me wanted to shout out, "Don't bother yourself! I don't like that stuff!"

Truth is, it was scary. It frightened me, but I couldn't say that. She would mock me something rotten if I said anything like that. "Mother the Mocker" I called her to meself sometimes. She was always taunting me about summat. But I knew better than to speak out, to cross her about that stuff. It was sacred to her, like reading the horoscopes in the Sunday Post. Nobody could persuade her against it. She swore by it and would have no truck with dissenters. So, I just throttled out a shrill "Okay mam" and rushed out onto the street.

I didn't like that dark stuff, witches and warlocks, ghosts, ghouls and dirty demons. I mean as kids we used to pretend, muck about and make up stories, specially at Halloween. But me mam and her brood they took these seances seriously, like it was real. Maybe it was. Maybe there were such things as demons. I couldn't see the good in it anyway. It made me shiver. I wondered if it was all those ghosts and apparitions they talked to that drove mother to those crazy outbursts of anger. Cos' it was just like some evil force would come over her.

No, that stuff was not for me! Not for me. Definitely not for me.

I slipped out into the street. It was as though I'd walked into a mildly tropical breeze, not so much the air, the atmosphere. The calm was tangible. I could breathe in, feel some peace. My spine stopped tingling. My tension subsided and the hairs on my head relaxed as I patted them down and put me cap on. It was nice out, but it was October.

I walked behind an elderly couple from up the road. It looked like they were off to church by the way they were dressed. People had a funny way of walking and talking when they were being all religious. I sometimes wondered if me ma was right about them. Whatever, they seemed a lot happier than we were, and gentler, mostly. Except for the caretaker, verger, whatever she was called; she was a grumpy old so-and-so if ever there was one. "The Tyrant in the Turban" I call her. She was from Lancashire.

The Tyrant in the Turban thought she ruled the world.

"Keep off that grass!" she would scream out as I passed by the cemetery. "Show some respect for the dead!"

What a funny thing to say, I thought. She doesn't seem to show any respect for the living. Why show respect for the dead? Still she was right though. We will all be there some day, dead and defenceless. I wouldn't want someone trampling over me.

I wondered what Yorkshire had done to deserve her. I began to get wound up just thinking about her. For reasons I didn't understand, she made my blood boil.

*'Don't think on that now, Robby me lad', I said to mesel. 'It just winds you up. Messes with your head. You don't want to spoil the fresh, cool, freeing air that's flowing through yer lungs now, do yer? You're a man now! An adult... You can deal with it!'*

*Yep, right, I want to enjoy life, don't I, not fret over daft twits like her all the time, or mother either for that matter.*

*Breathe in—breathe out.*

*Breathe in —breathe out, that's better, that's more like it. Breathe in – breathe out – breathe in – breathe out'*

*I felt my nerves settling down again. Hallelujah! Where did that hallelujah come from? Never mind. I'll go and see Chalkie and have some fun.'*

# 20. Collared by the Vicar

Just as I thought I was safely away from the house someone tapped me on the shoulder.

*'Oh my God!'* I thought as I turned around, hoping I hadn't said it out loud. It was the Vicar!

*'That's where that 'hallelujah' came from.'*
*I thought he was supposed to be in church doing his dressing up bit – getting into all them frocks he wears. What did he want with me? I hadn't done anything wrong. Maybe he'd heard I was in the pub last night and had come to warn me about the evils of the demon drink?'*

The Vicar was a funny guy. He was always a bit stiff and serious. He was tall and thin with hooked nose. He carried his head in the air like something was on the end of it - something smelly and unpleasant. He wore a dark suit all the time and a black shirt with a back-to-front white dog collar. He looked like he was going to a funeral.

"He's a bit glum looking," my dad used to say.

"Good to see you on your way to church this morning, young Rob," he says. He was cheerful enough. "Parents not coming along too?" He quizzed.

I stammered out a reply, indicating that I was off to visit a friend.

"Why don't you go later, after church?" he says. "You look as though you could do with some good spiritual guidance this morning."

*How did he know that?*

I wondered if he was a mind reader.

*'Have you been reading my diary'* were the words I wanted to come out of my mouth, but they stopped short before they reached my lips.

"I suppose I could, Vicar, if I'm allowed to come without my parents."

I said, trying to come up with another reason not to go.

"How old are you now, Rob?"

"Sixteen," I said full of pride. He caught me there. I should have lied.

"Of course, you can come on your own. You're officially a young adult if you are sixteen. Maybe it's time to start taking proper stock of the important things in life. Think for yourself. It does say in the Good Book, *'Remember your Creator in the days of your youth, before the days of trouble come, and the years approach when you will say, I find no pleasure in them.'* Time rushes on Rob, best start thinking about these things now."

It was a bit late for that. There were quite a lot of days that I found no pleasure in. Too many by my reckoning.

"Don't I have to wear a suit or get dressed up first?" I asked, still trying to find a way out of it.

"Well, of course, it is best if you do, but we understand if you are poor that it is not always possible. We can find you a seat at the back where you won't be noticed. God doesn't' mind how you dress, Robert. It's other people who have got airs and graces. I usually like youngsters to sit at the front so I can keep an eye on them, but I'm sure you'll behave now, won't you Robert?"

I wanted to punch him on his stuck-up, curled-down beak of a nose right there and then. When he said, *"We understand if you are poor,"* it made my teeth curl. I knew it was true, but there was something about somebody else saying it, and maybe him especially, that made me mad.

I managed to stuff my anger down and say nowt. I was saying nowt often those days. I must have had a ton of stuffed down anger packed in somewhere, with all the times I stuffed it down to keep the peace or save me lugs a bashing.

The Vicar didn't seem to notice my reaction, even though I was all but ready to bash him. Well not really, I wouldn't have done it, just in my imagination.

"Come just as you are, as we sing in the hymns, just as you are. Yes, come along with me. You'll be fine. I'll see you are looked after." He says, sounding almost human. Maybe he did read my mind after all.

I couldn't think of any other excuse. I felt trapped, so I gave in. I trudged down the road beside him the long five hundred yards to the corner of the street, then up the even longer alley and around another corner. There it was in the middle of the green. The sun was peeping through the grey clouded sky and a beam of yellow sunlight was shining over the graveyard in front of the church. I must admit, looking at it then, it was a handsome building with its bright, clean, sandstone walls, the majestic looking pillars at the entrance, and the stained-glass windows all around. Even the dark grey slate roof looked happy, contented, as if it was protecting the stone and wood and windows, overshadowing them like a hen with her brood of chicks.

# 21.  In the Church

We walked in silence, the Vicar and I alongside each other, till we passed through the great iron gate that guarded the entrance. Then we strode up the path before us to the main portico and through the church doorway.

"I'll get our new Curate Leonard to come and make sure you are okay," he said as we stepped into the auditorium.

It was light inside. There were rows and rows of dark mahogany pews with fancy cushions and kneeling pads. I didn't go to church often. Never on my own. Sometimes, rare times, when the whole street was involved, we would go along to the church hall, to the Bazaars, or the Pie and Peas Suppers. Those were the only times mother would come anywhere near the place. Different churches in the area had Street Processions throughout the year, most folks in the streets would join in, some got involved just for the fun of it, others like us would line the streets looking on, enjoying the drama and music and fancy dresses. On the rare occasions I had been into the building with the school for a service. I usually didn't notice much. I would have me head down, shuffle into my pew, get through the boredom as fast as I could, muck about with whoever was stitting next to me, wondering what it was all about.

Soon as it was over, we'd get out as quickly as possible.

But that Sunday, once inside the building it felt different, alive, like there was a buzzing in the air. As I looked around, I could see the great cathedral-like space was full of amazing things, glistening, ornate silver communion plates and a great imposing goblet upon a large oak table with carved legs, lush red carpets and gleaming brass railings across the front, and communion spaces where people went and kneeled down.

*'Wow! Wow!!!'* I thought as I looked around, noticing things for the first time.

God must be rich I remember thinking. This lot must have cost a fortune! Everything seemed shiny and fancy looking. Not like in the houses up our street. I suppose it was God's house, as they called it, and you wouldn't expect him to be short of a bob or two.

There was an aisle down the middle, pews either side, and two other aisles either side of them with shorter rows of pews. The sides looked full the first six or seven rows; the middle was half empty. Deep down somewhere inside me I felt a leap as we walked down the main aisle. It felt like it was a kind of welcome, a happy bump of lightness right where my heart was supposed to be. Or was it my liver?

Trotting down behind the Vicar, he stopped, turned round and ushered me into an empty pew about ten rows back on the left-hand side. There was nobody in the three rows in front of me. Maybe he had kept me back from the others in case I smelled or had nits or something.

"You sit there," he says, "and I'll get Leonard to come and see you are alright."

I didn't know what the time was, but I heard the church bells ringing out so I figured it must be near the start of the service. After a few minutes, they stopped, all was quiet. The shuffling stopped too. We were all waiting for something.

The organ broke the silence; it started up a deep droning melody. I was not a hymn expert, but I recognised the tune from school assembly: *'He who would valiant be, 'gainst all disaster, let him with constancy follow the master.'* I used to sing that old song every Friday for two years and would have been singing it still if I hadn't left school at fourteen. They wanted me to stay on to do continuation school to sixteen, but thankfully mam and dad agreed I could leave, said we needed the money, and I could get a job at Dorman Longs which would help.

All at once everybody stood up. I did too. I thought I'd better. A man in a long white dress I figured must be Leonard, walked down the centre aisle carrying a big book. It must have been the Bible. He climbed onto the platform and walked to the thing they preach from. He sat the book down on it and opened it up. He kind of bowed or half curtsied which I found a bit odd for a man. I mean there was nobody there to curtsey to, no Queen or King or whoever.

He sat down on the ornate wooden chair behind the pulpit. He was a thin-shouldered man, youngish, with a jaunty gait and friendly enough looking. He stared out into the crowd with a blank look as if he was seeing something nobody else could. Maybe it was God. The Vicar entered the sanctuary through the door to the left and walked over to the where the Bible had been put. The organ stopped. The Vicar grasped the wooden stand on either side with his outstretched hands, nodded down to it, looked up and began to speak.

# 22. Encounter with the Divine

"Please be seated," he called out across the church with his more than usual toffy-nosed voice. I wanted to punch him again, right on his beaky-pokey-out toffee-nosed snout. If there was such a thing as the Devil, he was raging inside of me right now. People talked funny in church, especially the Vicar it seemed. It made something inside me rise up. He dressed funny too. He wore a white robe as well, right down to his feet. He had a long green open waistcoat type thing with two big crosses in red at the bottom. He carried a wooden cross around his neck. There were a couple of rounds of rough green rope tied around the middle at his waist. I wondered why they got all dressed up like that. Maybe they were all poufters. Although I think the Vicar had got a wife.

'We'll begin this morning's service singing Hymn Number 3 from Hymns Ancient and Modern.' He read out the first verse...

*'Awake my soul arise and with the sun,*
*Thy daily stage of duty run,*
*shake off dull sloth,*
*And early rise,*
*to pay the morning sacrifice.'*

The organ started up, we all stood up and began to sing. The hymn came to an end. We were told to be seated, and he announced that he was going to pray.

Again and again his voice grated on.

"Let us stand and sing."

"Let us read from God's Holy Word."

"Let us pray."

"Let us take Communion."

"Let us have a moment's silence."

"Let us kneel and confess our sins."

It droned on and on in between the goings on for what seems like ages.

In the midst of it all came the dreaded sermon, during which I had planned to zone out cos I knew I would have no idea what he would be talking about.

"This morning's sermon is taken from that well-known psalm, Psalm 23. 'The Lord is my Shepherd'."

Well known?

I didn't go to church often, but I never heard them speak about any other psalm. I sometimes wondered if there were any others.

I was getting ready to switch off when something weird happened. It stunned me. If it hadn't felt so good, I would have said it was spooky. Peacefulness surrounded me. I was overwhelmed as this strange power blew over me like a gentle wind  of living, breathing air. I closed my eyes and let it carry me along. Opening them up I could see I had landed upon a distant shore, I had been transported to another world, a bright place, a large space of beautiful sights and heavenly feelings.

*'What on earth was happening to me? It all came upon me so quickly. I had no idea what was going on. What in heavens name had I let myself in for. No one told me this sort of stuff went on in church. It was incredible.'*

The exquisite feelings grew stronger and stronger. Every trace of anxiety, every angry feeling, disappeared. Vanished into thin air. In an instant, I shed all my heaviness, a ton weight dropped off my shoulders. I don't know how but every aching bone in my scrawny body had come to life. Every empty space in me was filled. Every sad and lonely feeling vanished. I was no longer sad, no longer alone. I mean I knew there were lots of folks in church, but it wasn't that, I mean I didn't feel lonely anymore. Injected with new life, and I felt like I was in heaven.

Ian had been right. If this was heaven, it was too marvellous for words.

Then I heard a voice, a soft gentle voice,

*"Jesus loves you."* The voice came calm and strong.

*"Jesus loves you,"* it said again.

*"Jesus loves you,"* it kept saying it again and again softly. I could see no one.

I was sure it wasn't the Vicar's or the new curate's voice; I don't know how, I just knew it.

*'God is love. His love is pure. His love is good. He fills the crushed and broken heart with healing ointment.*

Never in my life have I heard anyone speak like that. I was in a trance. I could feel love being poured into me like liquid honey—sweet, so sweet, I began to cry. I was so happy, so strangely happy. I couldn't ever remembered being as happy as that ever before. Every time the name Jesus was spoken, life welled up me.

It was so strong. I'd entered another world, become a different person. I wanted to answer back.

I had to say something. Then it just came out of my mouth.

*"Thank you."*

The words leapt out.

*"Thank you, Jesus. Thank you."*

I repeated it over and over again, hardly recognising that it was me saying the words.

I broke down, sobbing uncontrollable sobbing, sobbing from a deep place, crying from the depths of my stomach. I had never cried like that before. All the layers of sorrow, guilt, and shame I never realised till then were in there, bubbled up in a stream of cleansing water, and floated away. Layer upon layer of sadness lifted and what felt like warm liquid love flowed in to take their place.

I don't know how long I was there like that.

Time didn't exist anymore. It felt like eternity. I didn't care. I wanted to stay there forever.

# 23. A Narrow Escape

Out of the distance a different voice rattled in my ears.

"Are you alright lad?

A hand touched my knee.

"Are you okay?"

The voice sounded nearer and louder, bringing me out of that heavenly space, bringing me back to the irritation of earth.

I lifted my head and opened my eyes. A face stared back at me. I had no idea what to say.

"Who are you?" I managed to croak. My eyes were still blurry with tears. As they cleared and my senses returned, I could see it was the new curate. His hand was still on my knee.

"I'm Leonard, the new Curate."

I jolted upright and stepped back. Everyone else had gone.

"What's the matter?" he asked.

"Nothing. Nothing. I'm fine. Just got a bit overcome with things that's all."

Uncomfortable with this invasion of my space, this intrusion, this interruption of that incredible encounter, I turned away and headed to the other end of the pew. Something about the look on his face made me want to get away.

I ran up the aisle to the front portico.

The heavy wooden door wouldn't budge.

Panic surged through me.

I ran back down the aisle dodging past Leonard who was now standing at the end of the pew with a bewildered look on his face. There was a door to the side with glass panels. I could vaguely see someone on the other side. I pushed it open. It was the Vicar. Startled, he swung round, elbows in the air, half-way out of his cassock.

"What on earth?" he blustered as I barged past him to the door on the other side of the room. It exited onto the back of the churchyard.

Grabbing the big brass handle, I wrenched open the heavy door. Freedom beckoned. I gasped for air as I leapt down the two short steps to the gravel pathway, pulling the heavy oak door shut behind me, fully intending to hold back anyone who might pursue me. I heard it clunk hard.

I made my way out the back of the churchyard and circled round to the main street. Garnering my confused thoughts I decide to make my way back to Chalkie's house. It wasn't far, but far enough for me to think, to pull myself together. I walked on slower now, more composed, calming down.

I decide it was best to say nothing about these goings on. I needed more time to think, to process what had happened and figure out what it could mean. I passed a few folks on the street, some sitting, some standing in their open doorways, having a fag, supping a mug of tea or just watching their kids playing nearby. I smiled and nodded as I walked by them, still in a bit of a haze.

A hundred yards further on, I lifted the black metal knocker on Chalkie's front door and chapped three times. Their door was green, dark green. It was No 23. It needed painting. So did every door in the street. Except Mrs Sugden's that is, the young widow at no 27. Her door got painted fresh every year and her windows too. Her door was red.

"There seems to be no shortage of men volunteering to help her out one way or another," mother would say.

"I don't know where she gets the money to pay them,"

Truth is she took in lodgers, which wasn't unusual back then, many folks did. But there was no man of her own to be seen, in spite of being called Mrs. She was young and attractive, always nicely dressed and wafting the scent of old-fashioned roses, a common perfume of the day. She did have a habit of rubbing her hands on her hips though and had a look about her, when she talking with men.

# 24. Close Encounter of Another Kind

To my surprise, Elena opened the front door. "Oh, hello Rob," her smile beamed wide. *"What are you doing here?"* She asked surprised. I stood there not knowing what to say. I was suspended again in an emotional space between the volcanic outpouring in the church and the utter amazement at her welcome and the impact she made on me.

"Come on in," she said as confident as you like. I walked on in past her stopping a few steps into the hall. She glanced up and down the street. "Come away in,' she says again like she was expecting me. 'It's good to see you Rob." Still smiling she led me from standing there like a lemon in the hallway into the front room.

"Chalkie's out at practice and mam and dad aren't in just now. Me Gran has been taken poorly so they've gone to Redcar to see her. At death's door they say she is. I hope she is going to be alright. I like me gran. They made me stay home and look after the cat. It's due to have kittens any time now. I've got exams tomorrow as well, so I need to get on with me studies. If I'm going to be a proper nurse, I'll need to do well."

Elena turned sixteen five or six months before me, but she was always more grown up. Confident.

"I'm glad you're here anyway. I need to take a break for a bit. My head was getting scrambled with all that reading. I was just going to make a cup of tea. Do you fancy one?" She spoke as though we had known each other forever. I suppose all those years we'd played together as kids had created a bond between us. I figured that was it. But then there was those looks she used to give me over her mam's shoulder in the doorway as well. It had made me wonder if she felt like I did. And then there was that look as she passed by outside the pub that night when I went to fetch me dad.

"Yeh, that would be great." I said still trying to compose myself.

"You look flustered Rob, are you alright? What have you been up to this morning?" she asks as she walked into the narrow kitchen with the kettle she'd taken off the hob by the living room fire.

"Oh, nothing much, you know, just wandering around. I needed to get out of the house, things were a bit tense, with me mam and dad fighting again. Today it was a fight to see who could stay silent and sour-faced longest."

I watched her from the living room as she stood by the dresser. She took the tea cosy off the pot and poured the tea. If she was a magnet, I was helpless against the pull I felt towards her.

"Chalkie was telling me, it was your sixteenth birthday Friday. I saw him Saturday morning rubbing his lips with the toothpaste to get the smell of beer from his mouth. He was terrified dad would find out - but dad was in bed till late – he never knew. Poor Chalkie, he worries too much."

She came in with the tea. We sat opposite each other on the armchairs by the fireside; a right pair of grannie and grandads we must have looked.

She was lovely, even lovelier close up. I felt embarrassed, so close, alone, like this, the first time ever, I think. Since she left school two years back, we didn't hang about together anymore. And there were always other folks around if we bumped into each other in the street, or down the market Saturday mornings. I tried not to look at her too much, to stare, but I couldn't help it. She looked so grown already. Her neat auburn hair with the shiny clasp and I couldn't help noticing, she definitely wasn't a wee girl anymore. Her eyes twinkled even in the dim indoor daylight. I felt she was giving me glances every now and then as well. I hoped my cheeks weren't too red.

I was a bit shy to begin with to be honest, but we had a good laugh even though I did keep blushing. With her confidence I began to relax, and we gradually eased into each other's company, chatting and joking probably for the first time ever as *'grown ups'*. It felt so new and exciting. We talked about the past, days at school and playing around in the park. We talked about our mam's and dad's and Chalkie of course and her friends at the College, Marilyn and Christine. There seemed lots to talk about.

We talked about the here and now, new music, and the new dances and the cinema and films and the pub. We talked about our hopes for the future and the things we feared. We became so easy with each other. Looking back now it was a magical few hours like melting moments of fresh life bubbling up in the air around us.

As we chatted and supped our tea, we didn't notice that the fire had burned so low. She poked the fire and banked it up with more coal. We got off the armchairs and sat on the thin rug to draw closer to the heat. If we had only known how precious and beautiful but fleeting those moments were, we would have caught them up and stored them in a bottle.

After what must have been a few hours, the pregnant cat leapt off its chair in the corner of the room and started crying—to get out we thought. Elena tried to pick it up, but it kept running away.

We chased the poor thing around the room, scaring it half to death. I was surprised as it darted around so fast, out the living room and up the stairs even with a belly full of kittens. Elena ran up after it while I stood halfway up the stairs not sure about going up to the bedrooms. She scampered up, half on her hands, up the bare wooden stairs. As she turned to follow the cat into the back bedroom, she tripped on the torn lino on the top step and fell headlong with a great laugh. She was a fun-loving girl. Adventurous. It was surprising to me that she could be that way, unexpected when you think what her dad was like.

I was looking at her all the time, not that interested in the cat. She had on a light dress with green leafy and pink rosey flowery things, and pleats and a belt around the waist. I remember her waist. She was in white socks and slippers. As she fell, through instinct, I moved up to help her. She fell flat on her belly, her hands stretched out and her skirt lifted up in the fall. I just stared. I didn't mean to, but I couldn't help it. She turned over on her bum pulling her knees up to support herself. Her skirt had gathered up even more. She saw me staring at her and she blushed. I blushed more still.

She spoke, her voice teasing, as she straightened her legs out and pulled her skirt down. There was a glint in her smile, in her eyes as well. "Rob Fentiman! What do you think you are looking at? A gentleman would look away."

I blushed deep red again and didn't know where to look or what to say. She beamed having regained her composure and confidence.

I turned to head back downstairs, but she caught me by the arm.

"Come on!" she says. "Let's find that cat in case it has its kittens up here."

The cat was under Chalkie's bed which was set against the wall.

We were both on our bellies now, lying stretched out on the floor trying to get it to come out. "Come on kitty! Kitty, come on!" But it was too scared or too happy where it was to move. Cats go where cats will go.

Elena turned on her side in front of me. The laughing subsided, we looked at each other and were locked together in the moment, wondering, just laying, not moving, thoughts darting to and fro, eyes searching each other. Laying so physically close, we were vulnerable and she was irresistible. Excitement began to overpower me. I could feel her breath on my face and smell her sweet scent.

And that was it.

It happened.

Before we knew where we were, we were  tight together, kissing, holding each other close.

I don't know how.

Instinct took over. The instinct of passion, so powerful, driving the fumbling of youth through the frantic awkwardness to become one.

I was lost, we were lost in yet another kind of trance. We had stepped off this planet into unchartered territory, into bliss, newness. The adrenaline of excitement locked us together, quenching our thirsty souls with the flowing streams of each other's desire.

In what couldn't have been more than minutes, it was over.

We lay there semi-clothed, breathing, smiling at each other for who knows how long. Her hands clasped around my head, my right arm laying over her waist.

"Rob Fentiman! Well, I never! Happy Birthday or what!" she said with a bigger than ever grin.

We laughed. We laughed ourselves silly, struggling to pull our clothes on, only half embarrassed, only half trying not to look at each other, curious, shy still, but happy. I felt like I had crossed a threshold into a field of sensuous delight and walked through new pastures soaked with loves fresh dew. Maybe my old dad's philosophising ways had rubbed off on me too.

Feelings consumed me, fiery emotion swirled through my veins, *'Elena, Elena.'*

My mind was gone, and my heart was flying higher than a hot air balloon. My body had disintegrated into mush, barely held up by my skinny trembling legs. My face had been taken over by a grin bigger than a circus clown.

She looked at me close up with her now smoky eyes and put her hand on my cheek as we stood up. She kissed me on the lips.

She pulled back. She must have sensed something. She looked intently into my eyes and with the flick of a different switch she got serious.

"Don't you dare tell anybody about this Rob," she scolded. "My dad and mam would kill me if they found out. " I couldn't think of anything to say back, I was still lost in a haze.

"And Robert, I need you to promise you won't tell Chalkie either. He's just not good at keeping secrets. If you do, I promise, I'll deny it and you can kiss goodbye to the next time, you can be sure of that. I'll tell them you forced me."

Next time! She couldn't have said anything more divine.

I can't wait! I smiled back.

Just then we heard the sound of the front door opening downstairs and voices in the hall.

"Oh my God! They're back already."

"What time is it?" I whispered.

The clock on the bedside table told us it was five thirty. We must have been up there for hours.

# 25. The Great Escape

"I can't believe it's that time already. How am I going to get out? There is no way down the stairs without being seen or heard. I can't hide under the bed. I'd have to stay there all night. What if I run really quick down the stairs and out the door? They won't know it was me."

"No but they would know I've had somebody in my bedroom. You idiot! That won't work."

It's amazing how loving tones evaporate when fear shows up.

"Is that you Elena?" her dad's voice shouted up the stairs. "What are you up to? You're not in bed already, surely."

"No dad, I'm just getting the cat down, dad." She called back in a surprisingly confident voice, not a trace of my nervousness in her. "The cat ran up the stairs and hid under the bed. I was worried she might be hiding there to have her kittens. I'll be down in a minute. I've nearly got her."

"Elena, Elena" I whisper. "What am I going to do?"

"You'll have to go out the window," she says. "It opens out into the back alley. You can get away out there."

"But it's a twelve-foot drop or summat like that!"

I was terrified of heights, and I didn't want to break a leg either.

"Go on Rob. Go on. You'll have to. You can do it. There is no other way out. Unless you want us both to die tonight." She stressed, in a compressed whisper, boring her eyeballs into my skull as she spoke.

We crept over to the window, which thankfully was ajar.

Gingerly we opened it. I crawled out onto the ledge. Elena hung on to me as I manoeuvred my way out. I turned around, lowered my body down as far as I could, gripping the windowsill by my fingertips. I took a deep breath and let go.

The ground below rose up rapidly to meet me, putting an entirely new slant on that Old Irish Blessing, *'May the road rise up to meet you...'*

How they didn't hear the thud, or the gasping intake of breath as I hit the deck, I will never know.

I looked up. Elena was looking down to see how I was. She smiled a giggly kind of skew-wiffed smile and pulled the window back down.

Nothing broken, I scampered away up the lane, shaken in body by the ordeal, churned up just a bit by the fear, but higher than ever on excitement.

I headed home, my mind swimming.

What a day! What a day! As I raced up the road. I decided to take a detour. I needed more time before going in. I turned left a few houses up and headed towards the park. I found a bench and threw myself on it to think. A Kaleidoscope of thoughts and images flooded my mind.

What a day it had been. It certainly didn't turn out how I had imagined. I mulled things over, the events of the day tumbling still through my mind, how I managed to get myself collared by the Vicar, coerced into going to church, that weird thing that happened with God during the sermon. Maybe I shouldn't have said that Hallelujah walking down the street this morning. Then getting hit on by the curate, I think, maybe, I wasn't sure. I never did get to see Chalkie.

But then there was Elena. I didn't know if I should thank God for that or not. I'll never forget sitting with her by the fire, chasing the poor fat bellied cat up the stairs and the passion and terror that happened after that. The loving was, well, something else, but the great escapes were another. Not one but two, one escaping through the upstairs window in Elena's bedroom, the other, escaping from the wrath of Chalkie's dad.

I never gave a second's thought to God's wrath. Chalkie's dad was enough for me.

I knew this one thing for sure, Sundays would never be the same for me again.

# 26.  Just Another Monday

Monday morning came hard and fast. My workday alarm, dad thumping on the door, shook me back into this world at 6 o'clock. A quick wash in the cold water tap of the kitchen sink, a mug of tea, a chunk of bread, then it was out the door for 6.45.

Dad was leaning forward on the edge of his chair, clasping his hands around a mug of weak, milky tea. His eyes were screwed up, like he was straining to see something, glaring into the middle of the mug. His lips moved rapidly as if he was having a deep conversation with it. But no sound came out of his mouth.

He looked up when he realised, I was in the room.

"Time to get moving," he says, breaking off abruptly from whatever he had been thinking.

"Time and tide wait for no man. Are you ready to go?"

It would be years later before I learned, he had been praying into that mug of tea, a ritual he went through in his armchair every morning. He was praying to a God I couldn't see, and he claimed not to be interested in. I don't think he could see him either then, but like many, he just hoped somebody was listening.

My dad and I worked at Dorman Longs about twenty minutes' walk from home. He'd gotten me a job there when I left school. It was hard work, but it was all there was.

We left the house by the back door and joined the steady stream of men and young lads, walking down the road with their knapsacks packed with tea, and a few sandwiches probably jam, like ours.

Through the factory gates we swarmed, then up to the foreman's office to clock on before heading off to our various stations to carry out our given sentence for the day.

My dad was a stoker. He helped keep the furnace ovens going, shovelling coal all day long and clearing out the clinker and the ash. The ovens melted down the crude iron ore ready to be turned into long flat sheets of soft steel for making car bodies, oven casings and H beams for building work. Some of the iron was poured molten hot into great big ingots making cylindrical lumps like liquorice. They were cooled down till solid, then shipped off to different factories to be melted down again and made into other things.

Dad was in a gang of six, each man taking turns to keep the fires fuelled. They shovelled from the mountain of coal that came clattering through the trap door down the conveyor belt into the heart of the factory floor, waiting to be shovelled and wheel-barrowed and shovelled again into the red-hot blaze and the hungry flames of the greedy furnace.

My job was simple—to keep the floors swept and bring the men fresh water and clean towels, if you can call the rags they gave us that. So, there we all were, Monday morning, at work again.

Whilst my body had walked down the road with dad and my eyes had seen the men and the factory and my hands had clocked on and my ears had heard the foreman giving his instructions for the day, my mind and heart were a million miles away. I was lost in the turmoil of that long weekend. My imagination was flitting from one scene to another, remembering, reliving. I was still there. I was in my own internal cinema, images changing in my head in rapid succession, my brain was the projectionist, my heart the sound system, my whole weekend was the movie.

Friday night at the pub. The brass band. Mavis the *'lady of the night'*. Blood pressure rising. The Sally Ann lass. What was her name? The cockles and mussels fiasco, with me falling over the tables and making a fool of mesel. Back home and that murderous scene with me mam bashing dad with the poker, dad slumped over in the dunnie, frightening the life out of me, I thought he was dead. What on earth I would have done if he had been?

Saturday morning and scavenging coal and wood. Poetry lessons from Ian. The great concert at the bandstand in the afternoon. I loved that.

Sunday! What happened in the Church puzzled me still. So I tried to forget about it. It was hard to focus on the work. The memory of Elena and me entwined kept playing over and over in my head, got me so worked up, excited or anxious, I wasn't sure.

The new world of so-called manhood which opened up to me over that long weekend didn't just consume me for days and days, it followed me all through life.

The memories of Friday, Saturday and Sunday carved themselves into me. I was a lump of clay being moulded into shape; clay etched and ingrained with life-lasting scripts, grooves in my brain. Seeds of thought were implanted in me, tiny seeds that grew immense like jack and the beanstalk. Patterns of behaviour and thinking and emotions were stitched into the tapestry of life that were to define the adult me, the me who I became.

# 27. Somebody I Wasn't Meant To Be

But I became somebody I wasn't meant to be. I don't know how but I knew it made me into somebody that wasn't the real me. For years and even decades later, I felt like an old oil painting, a ruined masterpiece that had been covered over with dull brown varnish and had all but completely lost the technicolour of its original creation, its perfect design, the me I was intended to be.

The fear, the beer, the way of life, the false models of manhood, the stereotypes of women, all these things wrongfooted me... gave me so many red herrings and wrong principles and values upon which I built the future me, from which I carved out my rough existence.

A terrible fear of everything.

A fear that wouldn't let my mind do its intended job—to think properly, logically, clearly, wisely.

A fear that overpowered my skinny frame and affected my physical growth.

A fear that screwed my emotions, stunned me, drove me to stupid, self-destructive behaviour that bordered on madness.

I was confused. Confused about parents and God and men and women and love and lust.

Lust, that fiery Jezebel that fuelled a thousand crimes against my own soul and others.

Lust that chased me down the streets, haunted me at night and sowed its luring, lies and sucked me into its deadly embrace.

Confusion about what women were meant to be like. Was it my mother? My aunties? Mavis in the pub? Or Private Smith of the Sally Anne? Or Rosy Cheeks, the cheeky urchin with the cockles and whelks? Or the all-suffering housewife that was Chalkie's mum? Or Elena, Elena? They were not all soft and gentle and lovely for sure, not all sugar and spice and all things nice.

Yes, some were heaven in the flesh.

Others like beautiful roses, but with lethal thorns on their plump and slender stems. Some had piercing tongues and anger that could slice the bones and marrow apart, some were barely caricatures of once dignified humanity.

And there was the love of beer which gripped me in the second sip, hooked me and hauled me into its dark liar to devour me. The beer, the beer, oh the barrels and barrels, the depthless pools of that sweet nectar of the gods, that pint by pint would flow through my veins throughout the coming years. Is that what was meant to be a man – to be the greatest drinker in the world; to be a being whose goal in life was to be the first to drink the world dry?

But it wasn't just stupid pride in my capacity to consume.

The beer, that wicked tempting beer in whose vats I gladly immersed myself, became my escape from reality, my comforter, my saviour, the soother of my heart. When I drank, I felt good, calm, happier. It also destroyed my life.

And what did it mean to be a man. Was it my gentle, accommodating, timid, peace-at-all-costs dad? Was it Chalkie's grumpy, overbearing, irritable, hostile, fist flashing father? Those didn't-mean-no-one-no harm beer swilling men in the pub with all their mix of intriguing personalities?

What about that sleazy policeman masquerading as authority.

Then there was the confusing Vicar, or his questionable sidekick in some way modelling a peculiar version of a God, I may have met but didn't really know.

Which of these was supposed to make me the man that I was really meant to become?

I knew, I don't know how, somewhere inside of me, there existed a version of me with dignity, a purer, stronger fearless me, someone who could face the world with integrity, with honesty, someone who could hold his head up, the best version of me, a me who was struggling like hell to break out into the light of day.

All these thoughts swirled around in me as I pushed and pulled my stubborn broom to and fro across the factory floor.

# 28. Making a Living

There was a lot of sweat and dust in the blasting shed. It was dirty and thirsty work, but somehow satisfying – except strangely on payday. Everybody moaned on payday.

'All that graft' the men would say, 'and barely enough to pay the rent and put food on the table'.

It wasn't quite true, of course. Most men drank and happily smoked and gambled away some of that much needed money. Mother was always reminding dad about that, and that was what caused most of their arguments.

Most families had allotments to help eek the money out. Some kept hens so we would get a few extra eggs sometimes. One or two of the men kept pigeons. Not for food, but for racing mostly, unless things got really tight, in which case it was pigeon pie for Sunday dinner. Sad and Happy Days!

The allotments also attracted rabbits. They annoyed the gardeners but blessed the wives who were hard pushed to put food on the table. The pittance they had for food was like asking them to perform the miracle of the loaves and the fishes every week. That's what me mam said anyway. For somebody who didn't like church folk, she certainly knew a lot of Bible-type sayings.

Some of the men set snares along the wire fencing of the allotments. Not many weeks would go by without us having rabbit stew. I wasn't sure if we ate more food from finding it ourselves or from working at the factory. We would go along the hedgerows in summer and collect berries for jam and bottling. Whole streets went out. There were so many of us sometimes you had to walk for miles to find a spot where no one was picking. Thank God for the abundant generosity of nature.

Then there was the milkman's and the coalman's horse and cart, prized for their free supply of manure, if you were one of the lucky ones to get out on the street first. There was a bit of competition over it because some of the men didn't have allotments. But they'd still rush out and bag up the horse's dung. Then they'd sell it on to those who did. Desperate times meant desperate measures and sometimes daft dads. More than once or twice men came to blows over who got there first. It could be dangerous. They had shovels and weren't afraid to swing them around in a scuffle. Sometimes the drivers had to step in and referee.

"Scrapping over a bag o' dung are we, men? What's it coming to? Come on now. See sense, lads. There's enough to share."

Everything about life was a desperate struggle.

Our socks would get darned when they had holes. Shirt collars and cuffs were mended till they wouldn't mend any more. Clothes were handed down from one to the other as kids grew older and bigger. A man was buried in his wedding suit if he was lucky enough to have one of his own and not a borrowed one. Shoes were heeled and resoled at home in the back shed. They were cleaned every night, to make them last longer, or at least to look better longer. Most men had their own cobblers last, if not someone else in the street did, and they helped each other out.

Ours wasn't a cashless community, not quite but it was a bartering one. People swapping skills and sharing whatever they had to spare. Some of the women were good at baking bread so they'd bake for others in exchange for help.

"Necessity is the mother of invention," they would say. "Necessity is good for community life," me dad would say.

When he was feeling philosophical, dad talked about life. "It's like when it snows." You could tell when he was getting serious. He sat with his hands on his knees and leant forward just a bit, with a grave tone in his voice.

"With the snow, we all have a common foe we can see. When heavy snow comes and it's a struggle to get through the streets, it focuses all our attention and energy on survival. It's like that when you're poor. Poverty is like heavy snow; it pulls people together. The alternative is to fight like cats and dogs. Good community needs cohesive forces and challenges to thrive, so people pull together. It brings out the best in people. It does in these parts anyway, lad."

His voice was reassuring. He was a back street philosopher with the touch of the common man, who'd learnt his craft at the school of life.

"People value decency, honesty, helpfulness, sharing and respect. There are always rogues and chancers of course in any community, but the common weight of accepted values is basically good and makes you feel you want to belong together. All of us want what is best for us all. When people struggle to barely exist, there is something in the struggle that satisfies. There is a place in the souls of men that needs the muscle of struggle to be exercised. The drive to survive is a noble cause. Dignity comes not from the plenty, but from quitting ourselves like men in the challenges of life. You've got to man up, be strong and be of good character, lad. That's what matters in the end. What kind of a man have you been? Remember that son, as you get older.'

He paused. "Showing love to your neighbour is not just a nice religious sentiment. Without it, we would hardly survive. It's important to do right by each other. We need each other. And don't forget too, lad, in the end we have to answer to God, to the Judge of all men and women—aye, women too, thank God!"

I got some of what he meant even at my age, though the God bit was out of left field. I couldn't square it all with what went on between him and mother. I didn't have the nerve to ask him about that. Neither could I figure out why they complained so much on payday if it were okay to be poor and to struggle.

There was a lot about life I didn't understand. Why did they have Unions at the factory, for example? All they seemed to do was threaten to go on strike if they didn't get better pay, shorter hours or more holidays. The managers were always saying things were bad all round, the industry was in decline, there was nothing anyone could do, there was no more money to be had. That just made the men angrier.

"It's alright for them," the shop steward would say, "living in their fine bungalows and driving their flashy new cars while the rest of us live in poverty with rough wooden floor boards, a few scraps of lino, empty pantries and old clothes and us having to walk everywhere."

# 29. When All is Said and Done

Yes, we were back on planet Monday. Its misery hovered in the air. The excitement of my long weekend struggled to stay alive. Somebody should write a song. *"I don't like Mondays."* We'd all sing it.

By 10 o'clock Monday morning, we knew the weekend was over. Within hours of waking up and being at work, we were rebaptised in the factories oppressive air and drenched in the sweat of back-breaking labour. It wasn't long before those good memories and turbulent emotions, the good legacy of life's pleasures during that long weekend, were enveloped once again in the musty dust of the shovelling coal and the fiery furnaces of the iron smelting coke ovens.

And yet memories of the events of that long weekend were so indelibly fixed within me, woven into the great tapestry of my life, nothing on this earth could ever erase them. Their unique threads stretched far into the future to weave together the me that I was becoming.

*My, my Rob,* I thought to myself, *that was a long weekend that was.*

You'll not forget that one in a hurry.

Dad was right, war did come, and the world was turned upside down. Europe's fields were awash with blood once again. The lovely Elena and I wrote at least a few more pages of history with each other, a story in itself. Our so-called beloved streets were demolished, either by bombs or progress or politicians. The bricks and mortar of the Rivetter's Arms disappeared, but its stories lingered on in legend. The 'Smoggies', the peoples of that life, our friends, our neighbours and workmates were scattered far and wide, some moved into new estates built nearby. Dorman Longs survived though not where or how it was. Dad passed painfully away long before his time. Mother never died ever at least not in my mind. She lived on and on like a bitter sweet musical worm in my soul my whole life through, both enriching and tormenting me together, till at the very last I resigned my inner battle with her, reconciled myself with my past, with my memories. And I forgave her.

I eventually made peace with myself too, with the many good and bad, poor and rich players who had walked the boards alongside me on the universal stage of this often disillusioning, sometimes delightful little drama we call 'Life.'

Chalkie's heavy presence followed me throughout for decades. By the wonders of Providence himself, God used him to save me from at least one certain physical death. Friends, even heavy ones, are the lifeblood of living. Alone we are lost. Togetherness is where we belong, whatever we may be like.

Beer saved me too in its own way, but only for its own murderous plans, till with help I got the better of it in the end.

And so in the unfolding of my life, this was me. Then! Rob. Robert Fentiman, the me I was and the me I was becoming.

How it all panned out in the end is the stuff of stories yet to be told.

# Appendix

I have been asked many times, '*Why write this story?*' My answers are numerous. Life is a legion of complexity.

When I was 29, I realised I wanted a dad I could love, respect and relate to. Maybe this is just my way of fulfilling that need, tracing my roots to where it all began.

Rob is the name I used for my dad in the story; it's not his real name.

Rob is the hero, the central character, the point of the story—what he experiences in life—how it affects him and how it affects the course of his life—how the damaging experience of early childhood follow him like a shadow—and misdirects the better course his life could have taken.

The story is loosely based around early memories of things my dad spoke about. It is an attempt by me to discover who my dad really was—to view his life more fully, more widely with compassion—to rescue him in my consciousness—to understand how he became the person he did—to view him from a wider perspective than just a damaged human being and an alcoholic—to have a tangible dad in all his fractured wholeness that I could admire, or at least appreciate with compassion.

I have this belief that in some ways *'we are our ancestors'* so in seeking to *'know'* Rob, my dad, I am discovering something about who I am too.

As we are growing up many young people say, *'I don't want to be like my dad.'* Then as we grow up, we realise for better or for worse much of who we are is *'our dad'*.

Maybe the story is just what it is—Rob's life—make of it what you will.

With help and kindness we can love life, ourselves and others just a little more.

With kind regards to you, and thanks for walking with me through this part of the journey of Rob's young life.

T. D. Henderson